A LOVE REDISCOVERED

Mary Alford

Annie's®

AnniesFiction.com

Library of Congress-in-Publication Data
A Love Rediscovered / by Mary Alford
p. cm.
I. Title
                    2018945963

AnniesFiction.com
(800) 282-6643
Hearts of Amish Country™
Series Creator: Shari Lohner
Series Editor: Jane Haertel

10 11 12 13 14 | Printed in China | 9 8 7 6 5 4 3 2 1

1

Is it my imagination, or is the weather sending a warning? Ominous
dark clouds continued to gather outside, turning the late afternoon
to night. The snow fell even harder than it had that morning when
Anna Petersheim had arrived at the Latham ranch in Rexford,
Montana, where she worked as a housekeeper two days a week.

The thought of having to ride home in these worsening conditions
sent an unwelcome shiver through her.

"Why don't you let me give you a lift home, Anna? The roads are
going to be slick, and it's almost dark." Edward Latham, her kindly
English employer, must have spotted her nervousness.

As much as Anna would have loved to accept his gracious offer, she
could not. She needed to return her horse, Marta, and the buggy to her
community tonight. There was plenty of work to be done tomorrow,
and she'd need Marta's help.

Anna smiled at the elderly man's kindness. "That is very sweet of
you to offer, but it isn't necessary. I'll be fine. Besides, Marta knows
the road home well enough on her own."

That Edward would worry about her in such a way didn't come as
a surprise. In the nine months she'd worked for the Lathams, Edward
and his wife, June, had treated Anna almost like their daughter. She
loved them both dearly and was grateful to be employed by such
caring people. Each day, before Anna started her work, June would
invite her to have tea. While June was close to the same age as Anna's
mother-in-law, Mercy, they were from different worlds. June dressed

in slacks and colorful sweaters, but Mercy wore the district's approved gray or dark-blue calf-length dresses. Until recently, Anna had been required to dress in mourning black. The clothes might be gone, but the feeling of loss never would be. Her husband, Joseph, was dead. And he wasn't coming back.

She pressed the feeling down to a place inside her where it was more manageable and cast a worried glance outside. If she'd started out earlier, she'd be safely home with her *Dochder* by now. But today had been plagued with one delay after another. This morning, Sunshine, one of the family's two cows, had been uncooperative when Anna tried to milk her. Then, once she'd finished with the outside chores, Anna had wanted to make Chloe's favorite meal, chicken potpie. After an early lunch, her daughter had begged her to play a game with Fannie, the gently worn, faceless rag doll Anna's *Mamm* had made when Anna was a little girl. So it had been nearly one o'clock by the time she'd arrived here at the ranch. She had planned to keep a careful eye on the weather and leave before the day was so late, but she'd taken extra time polishing the silver, and the afternoon had slipped away from her.

"Are you *sure* you don't want me to take you home? I wouldn't mind." Edward's troubled gaze went to the windows, a worried frown on his normally jovial face. "The snow is really coming down hard out there. I'd hate it if something were to happen to you, Anna." In all the time she'd worked as the Lathams' housekeeper, she couldn't remember Edward ever being so persistent.

"I know you don't mind, but I'll be fine." Anna hoped she sounded more confident than she felt. She couldn't ask the man to make the trip home after dark. It would mean he would be traveling home alone in the bad weather conditions, and she'd never forgive herself if something happened to *him*.

She peered at Edward. He didn't seem at all convinced.

"You could stay here tonight. The guest room is always ready, and the storm should pass by morning."

Overwhelmed by his generous offer, Anna nonetheless shook her head. "Thank you, but Chloe is waiting for me at her *Grossmammi's*. She would be worried if I didn't come home." *And I have a quilt to finish tonight so I can deliver it to Mrs. Schwartz's Bulk Foods Store tomorrow.* Before long it would be completely dark. She needed to be home before that happened. "I really should be going."

Anna took her black cloak from the coatrack in the corner and slipped it over her gray dress and apron. Securing her traveling bonnet over her *Kapp*, Anna tucked an escaping strand of silver-blonde hair back into place, then donned her warm knit gloves.

As she said her goodbyes and stepped out into the late-afternoon gloom, Anna wished she felt confident about her decision, but she couldn't quite convince herself that she was. The sleet mixed with snow was pelting her already and her buggy wasn't enclosed. She wavered for a moment and glanced back at Edward, who stood in the doorway watching her.

Giving herself a mental shake, she realized she was behaving foolishly. It was only a few miles, and she'd promised Chloe she'd be home in time for dinner. Anna wasn't about to break that promise. Losing her *Grossdaddi* recently, so soon after her father's death, had broken the little girl's heart.

With a final wave of assurance to the elderly man, Anna went as quickly as she could to the barn.

She hitched Marta to the buggy and urged the mare from the barn's warmth. She'd made this trip dozens of times in similar conditions. What was the problem this time?

Apprehension pooled in the pit of Anna's stomach as Marta started down the driveway. She lifted her voice to *Gött*.

Please don't let me regret my decision.

The past year had been a struggle. They had almost lost the family farm that Joseph and his *Daed* had worked together. Even though years had passed since Joseph's unexpected confession that had led to his shunning, and after he'd worked so hard to repair the damage and regain the bishop's and the community's trust again, there were still those who only saw his sin. Their refusal to do business with him had added to the difficulty of making a living. Still, Joseph had never let his punishment get him down.

Anna forced aside those heartbreaking memories. Trusting Gött's plan for her life was sometimes hard, but she was determined to abide by the values her parents had instilled in her. She was surrendering her self-will to Gött.

Thick falling snow obscured the path in front of her. Where was the road? There were no other vehicles—Amish or English—in front of her to guide her. She wiped away the heavy flakes that stuck to her cheeks, leaving wet trails that made her exposed skin even colder.

I'd hate it if something were to happen to you.

She shivered and tugged the cloak closer for warmth. The cold of the mountains had a way of seeping in deep, right down to the bones. Anna wanted to get home as quickly as possible and see her daughter's precious smile once more.

Marta snorted. Anna stiffened and drew a sharp breath. Something had the mare spooked. Anna peered into the dense woods close by, but the storm and growing darkness prevented her from seeing anything. Springtime meant that the animals, awake from their long hibernation for months, were ravenous and ready to start feeding. Seeing black bears or mountain lions roaming the area wasn't unusual. Neither was ever a welcome sight.

"*Nay*, Marta." Anna held the reins tight and spoke in a soothing voice. "Everything is all right." Marta was not usually skittish, one of the things that made her perfect for Anna's needs.

With another careful look around for any would-be dangers, Anna eased the buggy around a tight curve, but then the horse stopped and pawed the icy road. Whatever the mare had spotted still troubled her. Anna shook the reins and Marta moved forward again.

Wind whipped around the mountainside with a renewed fierceness, carrying on it a different sound. As Anna braced against the gust, she heard what Marta had before. A vehicle was approaching from behind. The road's bend would prevent the driver from seeing her until the vehicle was almost right on top of the buggy.

Anna slapped the reins against the mare's flank. "Hurry, Marta."

The horse reared up on her hind legs, and Anna feared she would bolt. Using all her skills, Anna finally got Marta under control, forcing the buggy as far onto the shoulder as she thought was safe before the vehicle rounded the corner. She twisted around just as headlights appeared and pinned her in their beam.

The vehicle was almost right on top of her. There was no way the driver couldn't see her, especially with the buggy's reflective triangle, yet the car was heading straight for her at an alarming pace.

"Gött, help me." Anna barely had time to whisper the prayer before the vehicle slammed into the back of the buggy at full force. Wood splintered and Marta reared up on her hind legs again, then took off at a gallop, dragging the buggy through the snow along the side of the road.

Anna screamed and clutched the bench for support. Her gloved hands could barely hold on as Marta charged. Heart racing, Anna squeezed her eyes shut as the buggy shuddered and rocked along at a sickening pace. The damaged vehicle lurched, and Anna could no longer hold on. Her body left the seat, and there was nothing she could do to stop it.

She flew through the air. A lifetime seemed to pass before she hit the ground.

Anna's head bounced off the frozen earth, and her vision blurred. She tried to push herself up, but the pain in her right wrist was unbearable. She felt herself losing consciousness. *Chloe.* She couldn't bear the thought of dying out here and leaving her Dochder without a Mamm.

Anna saw a truck drive past, though she was unable to make out any details. She was too weak to try to flag it down. He must have seen the horse and damaged buggy. Why hadn't the driver stopped to help her?

A tear slipped down her cheek and she closed her eyes. Images of Chloe appeared before her. Her bouncing curls so much like Anna's own. Her beautiful brown eyes a constant reminder of Joseph.

Please, Gött, don't let me die out here alone. Don't let my Dochder have to bury her Mamm too.

The deteriorating weather conditions forced Noah Petersheim to keep his full attention on the icy road ahead, yet he was thankful for the distraction. He had less time to think about the reason why he was coming back home to his Amish roots.

Even after he'd had more than twenty-four hours to process the news, Noah still couldn't believe that his larger-than-life father was dead.

Not a year earlier, he'd buried his younger brother, Joseph. Now Noah was back in Rexford to say goodbye to his father.

He swallowed hard as guilt tore at his heart. After Joseph's fatal accident on a neighboring farm, Noah should have come home more often, or at least checked in with the family occasionally. He had used the excuse that his life as a CIA agent kept him out of the country for long periods of time, but that wasn't the real reason. He hated coming home because of all of the painful memories awaiting him here.

He'd walked away from Rexford and the Amish way of life when he was sixteen years old. Returning now, he was considered an outsider, an *Englischer*, by the people he'd previously called family.

Once upon a time, he'd loved everything about the plain life. That was before . . . It took everything inside of him to shove that memory aside.

He'd come home for only one reason. His family needed him. He'd stay as long as he could to help out his mother, and then he'd leave Rexford behind once more.

His father, Henry Petersheim, had been a pillar of the Rexford community. Now he was gone. His mother's letter had caught up with Noah after he'd returned from his most recent mission abroad. Too late to attend his father's funeral—another thing to be sorry for.

He recalled how solemn his younger brother's service had been. The great room of Joseph and Anna's home had been stripped of furniture to prepare for the first viewing. Only a handful of people from the community attended the two-hour funeral service. So many still held Joseph's former shunning against him.

The bishop had given thanks to God for His promise of eternal life, Noah hadn't been able to share in the thankfulness. There was bitterness in his heart.

Even though years had passed since Joseph's shunning ended, finding four friends to carry the coffin to the black horse-drawn hearse had been a difficult task. In the end, Noah and his father participated along with two local Amish men. Noah would never forget that day.

He recalled an old saying that was a favorite of his father's. *No winter lasts forever. No spring skips its turn.*

Noah wanted that to be true. But spring was still a long time from Big Sky Country, judging from the snow that was piling up all around him, even though it should have arrived by now.

Through the murky twilight of a cloudy late afternoon, everywhere he looked carried a wealth of memories, especially the times he and his brother, Joseph, had hunted and fished every square inch of the county, along with Noah's best friend, Adam Knepp.

Noah tightened his jaw as he remembered his friend and that dreadful day. His own foolish mistake.

Adam's death.

Noah shook his head, tightening his hands on the wheel. Shoving the dark memory aside was difficult, but he had to if he was going to get through this visit. He had to be strong for his mother.

Battle worn from the things he'd witnessed as an agent, Noah had endured enough pain to last him a lifetime. Dealing with his father's passing so soon after his brother's accident—well, the hurt cut deep. His mother deserved more than to be left with only him, the absent son.

Noah squinted through the snow flurries at the road ahead. He had struggled for a long time with his way of life, which conflicted with his Amish roots. Everything about working for the CIA went against his upbringing. He longed to call Rexford home again, but his past stood in the way like a roadblock. He'd been running from the ghosts of his friend's death and its aftermath since he was sixteen. In his mind, he wasn't fit to be called Amish any longer. So where did that leave him?

He eased around Henderson's Curve and struggled to keep the car from sliding into the opposite ditch. Once he had it under control again, he let go of the breath he'd held inside. This curve had been responsible for many accidents through the years. Some fatal.

Noah had barely cleared the curve when he saw a dark shape ahead. A buggy lay on its side at the edge of the road. The horse, bits of broken wood and leather straps still attached to its harness, stood nearby and was clearly agitated. The wreck appeared to have just happened.

Noah slowed gently, but on the icy roads the back tires locked up and the vehicle spun sideways. He managed to bring the car to a stop in front of the horse and buggy, then grabbed the flashlight out of his bag and slipped it into his jacket. Snow pelted him as he approached the accident scene.

When he reached the buggy, it was empty. Had the owner escaped unharmed and gone for help? In these freezing conditions, he would never make it to Rexford.

"Whoa there." Noah did his best to calm the animal by stroking her muzzle. The mare fought him, pawing at the ground. When he'd finally settled her down, he disentangled the horse from the leather and splintered wood and led her to a nearby tree, where he tied her up. Maybe a little distance from the wreck would soothe her.

Where is the driver? He surveyed the scene, snow periodically blinding him. The wind died down momentarily and he heard something. A groan? He spun in the direction he thought the sound was coming from.

Something covered in black fabric lay near a tree about twenty feet from the buggy. Noah trudged toward the figure as fast as he could. When he reached the motionless body, he shone his light on the face, which was half-buried in the snow.

A stab of panic hit him. He knew this woman.

It was Anna, his brother's widow.

Noah did a quick examination of her limbs, as well as he could while holding the light. Nothing appeared broken, but without X-rays he couldn't be certain. One wrist was swollen, and it would only get worse. Blood colored the snow near her head, having seeped through both her Kapp and traveling bonnet. Fear spiraled down into his gut.

Anna could have unseen injuries that needed immediate medical attention. And every minute in the freezing cold would increase her chances of hypothermia.

He shook her gently. She didn't open her eyes.

He pulled his cell phone from the pocket of his jacket, but he wasn't surprised to see he had no service. He needed to get her to the car and take her to the nearest hospital.

Slowly, he eased her into his arms and rose to his feet. She felt so small. He'd known Anna most of his life. The young girl who used to follow Noah and her brother Adam around everywhere had grown into a lovely woman. Yet the past year had taken a toll. Smudges beneath her eyes spoke of sleepless nights. Even unconscious, an expression of grief appeared branded on her face.

Noah carefully picked his way through the snow to the car, doing his best not to jostle her. Once he reached the car, he managed to open the passenger door, and as gently as he could, placed her inside the warmth of the vehicle.

Before he could close the door, Anna's eyes flew open. Her startled green gaze latched onto him, freezing him in place. She clutched his arm with her uninjured hand, clearly terrified.

Noah did his best to reassure her. "Everything is okay. You were in an accident, but I think you are going to be fine. I need to take you to the hospital to make sure you don't have any internal injuries."

He barely got the words out before she shook her head, rejecting the idea completely. Her hand still clutched his jacket. "I can't. I have to go home. Chloe will be worried, and I promised her I would be home for dinner. She's counting on me." She drew in a breath. "I don't need a hospital. I need to get Marta and the buggy back home."

Her courage reached to the part of him that he made sure no one ever saw.

"You're hurt, Anna. Your wrist is swollen, and your head is bleeding. There could be injuries we can't see. You must have medical attention." He gently touched the back of her head, searching for the wound. Her breath caught and he immediately jerked his hand away. He'd been too forward. She was an Amish woman.

"You can use the community phone to call Dr. Montgomery once we're home. I won't disappoint my *Kind*. She has been through enough this year."

Against his better judgment, he nodded. "I will take you home. In the car. And we'll find some men to come and take Marta and the buggy home. She's tied up in the shelter of those trees down there, and the snow looks like it's letting up. She'll be fine."

"No." The tone was weak, but defiant. "I'll drive the buggy—" Her head turned from the wreck, toward Noah, and she deflated. "Even if we managed to right it, it isn't safe to drive, is it?"

"I'm afraid not." Noah waited, hoping she would make the right choice on her own.

"All right. Thank you, Noah."

He took it as a good sign that she had not only agreed with him, but recognized him. He could only pray that *he* was making the right decision by not taking her directly to the hospital. The warmth of the car seemed to help ease her shivering.

Thank goodness she had given in, perhaps realizing she was in no condition to protest. And he had to admit to himself that, although he wouldn't have wished such an accident on his worst enemy, he was grateful that he didn't have to return to his Daed's house alone.

"How are you feeling?" he asked as they pulled out onto the road to Rexford. From the corner of his eye, he saw Anna settle back against the seat.

"I'm all right," she said, though she sounded anything but.

"What happened back there?" Noah asked. Anna had been driving a buggy since she was young. She was more than capable of handling whatever Marta's temperament might bring, even in a snowstorm, yet there had been a great deal of damage to the back of the buggy.

"What's wrong?" he prompted.

"Nothing . . . I'm not sure." She hesitated, her focus on the road.

"Anna, what happened?" He didn't like the feeling that pooled in the pit of his stomach.

She drew in a breath. "There was a vehicle." She started shivering again.

He covered her good hand with his for a moment, then returned it to the steering wheel.

"Noah, I think someone hit me on purpose."

2

"What makes you think that?" The question was sharp, his concern evident in his voice and in the hard set of his jaw.

Why *did* she think it was intentional? Her thoughts had been fuzzy after the fall, perhaps still were. Maybe the driver simply didn't realize he had hit her buggy—but that was ridiculous. It was not yet fully dark outside, and it was impossible that the driver had not seen her or felt the impact with the buggy. Yet the thought of someone wanting to harm her was a difficult one to accept. She knew almost everyone who lived in the surrounding area. She had sold many of her quilts and wall hangings to the English at the annual Rexford Amish Community Auction and done business with them in town. They were all good people. Certainly no one would do such a terrible thing for no reason. Her heart wouldn't let her go there.

"I spoke without thinking. I'm sure this wasn't on purpose. Perhaps the person who hit me drove on to Rexford to bring back help." Even that wasn't especially reassuring. The image of the vehicle leaving the scene rose in her mind.

Noah shot her a narrowed glance. "The driver must have known they'd hit something. Why didn't he stop to check it out?"

Anna could not supply an answer. Noah was right. The driver must have known. And anyone from the community would have stopped. Unless they were too scared—a thing she understood very well.

Her head ached where she'd hit it on the ground. She touched the spot and winced. Blood had seeped through her traveling bonnet.

Her swollen wrist was painful to the touch. Her apron had torn in several places, and her cloak was damp from the snow. She must look a sight. Anna couldn't imagine how Chloe would react to seeing her Mamm like this.

Anna clenched her good hand into a fist, struggling past the tears welling in her eyes. She would not cry in front of Chloe—or Noah. She'd be strong.

"How are you feeling now?" Noah glanced at her, and in his eyes was the same compassion she'd seen on the day they had buried Joseph, bringing with it a wealth of heartbreak. Rain and tears filled that bleak day. Her heart had broken into a thousand pieces as she watched her husband's simple pine coffin being lowered into the ground. Would her heart ever be whole again?

"I am okay." But she couldn't meet his eyes when she said it. She ached all over and was starting to feel dizzy and a bit queasy. All she wanted to do was lie down and sleep for days.

Anna drew in a deep breath and some of the fog in her mind lifted as they topped the final hill. The community of Rexford spread out before them. As always, a sense of peace and happiness swelled in her chest. In spite of all the heartache she'd endured in her life, she couldn't imagine living anywhere but here. This was home and always would be.

As Noah steered down the snowy street that cut through the middle of town, Anna cast him a sidelong look. He had been gone from his home for years, had chosen the English world over the plain life. Did he have regrets?

Noah was a handsome man. He and Joseph were alike in many ways, yet different as well. Noah wore his thick, dark-brown hair cut short. Nothing like the youth she remembered all those years ago. He was no longer the same carefree person who'd left Rexford behind at sixteen.

His mother kept up with Noah mostly through letters. Mercy told the family about his life in the dangerous world of the CIA—or as much as she knew, anyway. She worried about her elder son constantly and prayed for his return to the simple life one day. Anna hoped her prayers would be answered this time.

As difficult as his absence was on his family, Anna understood all too well why Noah had left at the time. He and her brother Adam had been as close as kin. Noah had taken Adam's death very hard.

When the silence between them stretched on, she said, "Your Mamm will be happy to see you." Noah was all Mercy had talked about since she'd received the word he was coming home. "She misses you. She might not say so, but she does."

He visibly swallowed and kept his eyes on the road. "She wants me to come home for good. She doesn't understand that isn't possible and never will be."

Shock rippled through Anna at his declaration. She wasn't sure how to respond. "If you want to come home, you should. Adam's death was a long time ago. Maybe you should let him go."

He shook his head. "My Mamm doesn't understand," he repeated, reverting easily back to the language. "I'm not part of this world anymore, Anna. The community won't accept me. Not that I blame them." A hint of disgust tinged his words.

She wished she could deny it, but what he said was true. Even though he'd grown up here, Noah hadn't joined the church. Instead, he'd chosen a life apart from the community. He was an outsider.

Against her will, she thought about Joseph's shunning. He had been terrified that Anna would turn her back on him as well, but she hadn't. How could she when she loved him so much?

While to the outside world the act of shunning a fellow member of the community might seem cruel, it was necessary to maintain order for the Amish. The tradition might not be kind, but the community respected it.

She studied Noah's stubborn countenance. Nothing she could say would change his mind about staying. Instead, she kept her eyes trained on the road ahead as he drove out of town toward the Petersheim farm.

The accident replayed in her mind, the car speeding on a direct path into the back of her buggy. She hoped she was mistaken about the driver's intent, but she couldn't shake the feeling. She recalled Edward Latham's earlier concerns, although his had been about the weather, not someone deliberately ramming her buggy. But she was alive. The accident could have been far worse. She would remain thankful that Gött had spared her life.

Still, there was no denying that the Petersheim family had experienced more than a few accidents lately. Was it possible that two people were dead—her husband and now her father-in-law—and that she had narrowly escaped with her life all because of *accidents*?

Noah swallowed hard, but the lump in his throat refused to go away. Being back in Rexford brought back good memories along with the ugly ones, ones that refused to lay hidden any longer.

Time seemed to stand still here. Everything about the place was the same as when he'd left for good. Beiler's Bakery on the right. Weaver's Handcrafted Furniture across the street. Mrs. Schwartz's Bulk Foods Store next door. How many times as a child had his Daed sent him to Mrs. Schwartz's to buy supplies? Or his Mamm would have him pick up a loaf of fresh-baked bread at Beiler's for the evening meal. Yet all those warm memories were poisoned in a single day—the day Adam died. Now he would forever associate his former home with death. First Adam, then Joseph. Now his Daed. All gone before their time, and he couldn't keep the bitterness in his heart from rising to the surface. He blamed himself for Adam's death. Gött was responsible for the rest.

As hard as he tried, Noah still couldn't imagine standing in his family home and not seeing his Daed's smiling face.

When he had reached his mother through the community phone in town after learning of his Daed's passing, Mercy refused to discuss the details of what had happened to her husband by phone. All Noah knew about his Daed's passing was that it had been caused by an accident.

Like Joseph.

What had happened to Anna tonight hung heavy on his thoughts. While she didn't want to believe someone had deliberately run her off the road, in Noah's mind, that was the only explanation even though he didn't understand why. He had been around Henderson's Curve many times in a buggy and in a car. Despite the bad weather conditions, the driver should have been able to see Anna's buggy in time, especially with the reflective triangle.

Was he simply being paranoid, his current life bleeding into this simpler one, or was something strange going on in the Rexford community?

Up ahead, Noah spotted his family home. The pale glow of lanterns inside lit the way like a beacon in a storm. A storm certainly raged inside of him. Noah had tried so hard through the years to convince himself that he'd left this part of himself behind, yet no matter how hard he tried, he couldn't purge it from his heart.

The lights of home reminded him of all the times past when he'd returned from working the field, and his Mamm would have supper sitting on the table, waiting for her family. Whenever he was out on a particularly dangerous assignment, his life on the line with threats coming from all sides, he'd close his eyes and this image would come to mind. The peace he felt remembering his family home had helped him survive countless difficult situations.

Noah pulled into the driveway and stopped in front of the house. As he stared up at his family home, breathing became difficult. He could almost picture his Daed coming out to greet him. The emotional pain only intensified. He hadn't dealt with the past—he'd simply run away. Maybe now was the time to make peace, once and for all. Or try to, anyway.

Anna shifted her face toward his, questions he didn't want to answer in her eyes.

He exited the car before she could voice any of them.

After opening her door, he held out his hand to help her out of the car. Their eyes met. She inhaled deeply, as if steeling herself. Then she took his hand and let him guide her out of the car. She let go as soon as she was upright.

"Let's get you inside," he said. "I'll get the doctor's number from my Mamm and make the trip into town to the community phone."

Anna turned away, about to trudge through the thick snow, when she stumbled. He caught her arm.

"Careful now."

Her soulful eyes looked on him with a deep sadness, but also with a strength he admired. Joseph had been a lucky man to call her his. She deserved only happiness in her life. Instead, death surrounded her.

The moment she was steady on her feet, he released her. She was under five and a half feet tall, petite and pretty, but she wore her grief like part of her mourning clothes. And he suddenly wished he could take her pain away.

Noah opened the door for Anna and followed her inside.

"Anna, where have you been? I was worried—" The moment his

Mamm spotted him standing behind Anna, she halted midstride, almost as if she couldn't trust what she was seeing. "Noah?"

He smiled at her shock. "Yes, it's me, Mamm."

The love shining in her eyes humbled him. He didn't deserve it.

"Noah." Mercy ran into his open arms and hugged him tight. "Oh my *Soh*. You're finally home."

Noah wished that he shared in her happiness as he held his Mamm while she cried tears of joy. He would give anything if he could be happy that he was home again. To make her wishes come true and stay in Rexford forever, as his heart clamored to do.

When she pulled away, her eyes brimmed with love and a smile brightened her face. "I was afraid you wouldn't come."

Her words broke his heart. He didn't know how to answer her. He was here out of obligation. Nothing more. And he already regretted the decision.

But this talk was for another day. Right now, Anna needed help. "Mamm, Anna is hurt. She was run off the road tonight by a vehicle. I need to find someone to go bring her horse and what's left of the buggy home. And to call Dr. Montgomery to come examine Anna."

Mercy hurried to Anna's side. When she got a good look at her daughter-in-law, she clasped her hand over her mouth. "Come lie down. You're ready to drop on your feet, and your wrist . . ." Tears sparkled in Mercy's eyes.

"Mamm!"

No one had noticed the little girl standing in the kitchen until she spoke. Noah turned at the sound of the tiny, panicked voice. She stared at her mother, eyes wide with terror.

Anna held out her arms to her daughter. "Chloe, I'm all right."

The little girl ran into her Mamm's arms. Anna flinched in pain, but squeezed Chloe close with her good arm.

Tears streamed down Chloe's face as she peered up at her mother. Anna's smile was clearly forced. "See? I'm fine. A few cuts and scrapes. Now, no more tears."

But Chloe kept crying and buried her face in her mother's dress, so Anna held her close, murmuring soothingly. The sight tugged at Noah's heartstrings.

Mamm's voice shook him out of his reverie. "Noah, Dr. Montgomery's number is in the kitchen cabinet. Go call him as quickly as you can. And stop at the Yoders' next door. Carl and his sons can go fetch the horse."

Noah found the number and headed for the door. The picture behind him of mother and child was an innocent reminder of the things that would never be his. A family like theirs was not in his future. Once he'd made sure there'd be someone to help with the farm, he would return to his life as a spy. But the thought of what lay ahead for him was growing less appealing with each new mission. He forced his gaze away from the display of love before him and trudged out into the snowy Montana night, drawing in deep breaths of fresh mountain air. His emotions were all over the place today. Coming home to Rexford had opened wounds that were best left untouched.

Facing what was to come when the truth about his Daed's passing was revealed was like staring into the great unknown. Memories of Henry had filled the house when he was inside. Noah could still picture him sitting in front of the woodstove, reading the *Biewel*. Henry Petersheim had lived his life guided by the Word of Gött. No matter what trouble came his way, he had prayed first and turned to the Bible next. Noah remembered coming home to be with his family after Joseph's funeral. Few words were spoken that day. His Daed had immersed himself in the Bible from the moment they reached Anna's house until bedtime.

Noah shook off the memories of that dark day. He'd rehashed each moment in his mind dozens of times, and it never did any good. And wouldn't now.

After stopping next door and securing a promise that Carl Yoder would retrieve Marta and the buggy, Noah drove back into town. While the community members of Rexford were prohibited from owning modern technology, the bishop did allow for a community phone shanty, which was a couple of blocks from the bakery.

Out of respect for his family, he had chosen not to use his cell phone, though the gesture seemed silly now. He wasn't part of this community anymore and never would be again. What difference did it make? Still, this felt like the right thing to do. If this had been an acute emergency, he'd have made a different decision.

Once he reached the shanty, Noah pulled to a stop, then retrieved the scrap of paper from his pocket. Not a single light shone in town. The Amish rose before daylight and went to bed early.

The English doctor who served the Amish community answered on the first ring.

"Dr. Montgomery, this is Noah Petersheim. I'm calling for my sister-in-law, Anna." Noah explained what had happened on that lonely road earlier in the evening.

"Another accident!" The doctor's voice was full of concern. "And Anna was run off the road, you say? Unbelievable. Everyone around the community is always so careful." The doctor clicked his tongue. "I have never seen a family plagued with so many accidents as yours, Noah. One is an accident. Two is strange. Three . . . is something far worse."

The doctor's confirmation of his own feelings struck hard. He didn't know how to answer. Thankfully, he didn't have to.

"Tell your mother I'm on my way there now. I'll see you all soon."

"I will. Thank you, sir." Noah hung up the phone and returned to the car. Dr. Montgomery's words settled around him like a dark cloud. The man was right. The accidents surrounding his family were beginning to mount. Was it all a strange coincidence, or was it something far worse, even sinister?

Noah couldn't make sense of someone coming after his family deliberately. His Daed had been an honorable man without an enemy around as far as he knew, and Anna was loved by everyone in the community. Surely the events that happened all those years ago had been all but forgotten. No one could still blame Joseph for Adam's death enough to hurt his family, could they? That wasn't the Amish way. They were a humble people who didn't believe in vengeance. Forgiveness was easily given. *Except to me. I don't deserve it.*

He'd talk to his Mamm and find out what, if anything, she was keeping from him about his Daed's death. Maybe this would prove to be just a series of accidents after all.

Noah flipped up his coat collar against the biting Montana chill. He wanted to get back home and make sure Anna was okay. With his Daed's death, Noah's family needed him, at least for now. But he couldn't stay forever.

3

"You're lucky nothing was broken, Anna. That was a nasty fall you took." Dr. Montgomery finished bandaging her sprained wrist, then carefully cleaned her head wound.

Even now, though she was safe at her mother-in-law's home, Anna couldn't stop trembling. The accident had been terrifying, and the memory was just as vivid.

Noah stood off to the side, silent and out of the doctor's way, but watching intently.

She forced herself to put on a brave face. "It wasn't luck. I was in Gött's hands, as I always am." She stood, then closed her eyes and staggered as the room began to spin.

The elderly doctor clutched her arm to help steady her. "Easy now." He used a soothing tone. "You need to rest. That injury to your head was bad."

Once the world settled down and her stomach calmed, she opened her eyes and tried to reassure Dr. Montgomery that she'd be all right. "Thank you for coming so quickly."

He patted her arm. "You are like my daughter. I've been watching out for you since you were a little girl. That will never stop."

She smiled up at him gratefully. Even though Dr. Montgomery had retired from private practice several years earlier, he never failed to help the community whenever the need arose. He had been the one to respond to Henry's recent fall and had ridden in the ambulance to the hospital with her father-in-law. And Dr. Montgomery had pronounced Joseph dead on that horrible day.

"I remember, and I'm thankful for everything you've done for me and my family."

His eyes shone with compassion. "As always, you are very welcome. But don't do anything too strenuous for a couple of weeks. That means no housework. Edward and his wife will understand," he added when she frowned.

Hearing that she wouldn't be able to work for two weeks did nothing to ease her troubled thoughts. How would they make ends meet without the extra income? She glanced at Noah, who stood, arms folded, stoic as a sentinel on guard duty.

"From what I can tell, you came very close to breaking that wrist tonight. If you put too much strain on it, the wrist may not heal properly." Dr. Montgomery addressed Mercy. "Keep an eye on her. She has a mild concussion. If anything changes during the night, call me right away. No matter the time."

He retrieved his hat and coat from next to the door. "I should be on my way. Virginia worries when I'm out after dark. Speaking of, you shouldn't be traveling alone so late anymore, Anna. As I said, you were very lucky this time. Next time, maybe not so much."

Mercy showed the doctor to the door. "Thank you again, Dr. Montgomery. We are always grateful."

He gave Anna another smile, then tipped his hat to Mercy before heading out into the chilly night. A few minutes later, his car engine started up, and then he was gone.

The reality of what had almost happened sank in. Anna was so grateful that Noah had come along when he had. If he had preceded her or come on a different night, she might have lain in the snow for hours. She didn't want to think about what might have happened.

Chloe had fallen fast asleep on the sofa, covered by a warm, soft quilt that Anna had made last year.

Anna dropped a gentle kiss on her daughter's head. Until this moment, she hadn't considered where Noah would sleep now that he was here. She and Chloe had been staying in Noah and Joseph's old bedroom since Henry passed. Anna had been taking care of the chores around her own home after she helped Mercy with hers. Having family close was good for all of them.

"Let me make you something warm to drink." Mercy brought another quilt from the chest close by and placed it around Anna's shoulders. She suppressed a smile as Mercy hurried away. The gentle woman had been fussing over her since she was a young girl, and now that she was a grown woman, Mercy still seemed to take pleasure in it, perhaps because she'd never had a daughter of her own.

Anna had married Joseph soon after losing her own parents when she was barely eighteen. She'd come to love Henry and Mercy as her own. Mercy had taken her under her wing and become like a second mother.

"Hot chocolate. Good for soothing away the chill." Mercy sat a steaming cup on the end table beside her and handed one to Noah.

Anna clasped Mercy's hand in her good one, forcing the woman to look at her. "Noah will need a place to sleep. Perhaps Chloe and I should stay at our home tonight."

Noah was quick to reassure her. "I'll be fine here on the sofa. I don't need much room. Besides, you have to rest, and Mamm needs to keep an eye on you. You heard Dr. Montgomery's orders. You have a concussion."

Anna hated putting him out in such a way. His tall body would be cramped on the tiny sofa. But Noah was a man of honor. He wouldn't take no for an answer.

The hot chocolate warmed her inside as the quilt warmed her outside. Finishing the last of the drink, she set the cup down and rose to her feet. The world around her was still out of focus, and she was beginning to feel even more of the effects of the accident. Her body ached.

Noah steadied her when she wobbled on her feet. "Are you all right?"

She nodded and pulled away.

"You need food, and then rest," Mercy ordered.

Anna knew she would be foolish to argue with Mercy once she'd made up her mind. "Yes, but only for tonight." She lifted her chin. "Tomorrow, Chloe and I must return to our own home now that Noah is here." Anna thought about the quilt that still needed to be finished along with the wall hangings she had planned to deliver to Mrs. Schwartz's store the following day. Now, all that would have to wait.

Mercy seemed to read her thoughts. "Noah can take you to the store tomorrow. You can finish the quilt when you are feeling better." To Noah, Mercy explained, "Anna sells her lovely quilts and wall hangings at Mrs. Schwartz's Bulk Foods Store. She was planning to take some to the store tomorrow."

Noah peered into Anna's eyes, and her cheeks grew warm. "I can drop them off for you. You should stay home and rest," he told her.

"*Danki*, but I will be able to make the trip to the store just fine. Dr. Montgomery said the sprain wasn't so bad. And my head will be fine."

Noah clearly didn't agree, but he didn't argue. "Suit yourself." The tone was clipped, professional.

Mercy didn't seem convinced either, but she said nothing.

Anna glanced down at Chloe. She hated to wake the sleeping child, but she needed to get her daughter upstairs to bed.

"Here, let me." Noah gently lifted Chloe. She wrapped her arms around his neck as she had so many times in the past with her father and later her grandfather. Noah froze for a moment, apparently shocked.

Then he slowly carried Chloe to his old bedroom while Anna followed behind, wincing with each step.

Noah carefully laid the child on the bed. Chloe rolled onto her side as she always did, and Anna stroked her Dochder's soft curls. Chloe made her life and heart full. Anna was blessed beyond measure.

She slipped from the room followed by Noah, leaving the door open a crack in case Chloe woke and grew afraid as she sometimes did. With Henry's recent death, the girl's world had crumbled once again, and her anxiety had grown.

In the kitchen, Mercy had a light meal waiting for them on the table. "Come and eat, both of you. You two must be starving." She dished out two bowls of beef soup along with some of her crusty homemade bread.

Anna realized with surprise that, in spite of everything, she was hungry. She focused on the man by her side. Joseph, his brother, had taken after Mercy with his blond hair and brown eyes while Noah had Henry's darker hair color. Nothing about Noah's appearance, from his short hair to his jeans and sweatshirt, spoke of his plain past.

Noah hugged his Mamm tight. "You're right. I am starving, and this smells wonderful."

Mercy's cheeks grew pink at her son's compliment. "Sit. The food is getting cold. And cold soup would be such a disappointment on a night like this."

Anna watched the two of them together and couldn't remember the last time she'd seen Mercy so happy. All because of Noah's return. What would happen when he left Rexford again? She prayed it wouldn't be too much for Mercy's battered heart to bear.

Mercy sat down next to her son, her eyes sparkling with joy. Anna wouldn't think about the future right now. Seeing some of the sadness eased away by Noah's presence was enough for the moment.

Anna bowed her head for the silent prayer. From where she sat, she could feel Noah's anxiety. When she finished her prayer, she noticed him watching her. He didn't bow his head. Did he still remember their ways?

Eating with her left hand was a challenge, yet the throbbing in her right wrist made using it impossible. She got down a little of the soup, but the pain dulled her appetite and she pushed the bowl away.

"You hardly touched your food," Mercy said with concern. "Are you hurting?"

She slowly nodded. "Maybe a little."

"You should take the medication Dr. Montgomery left for you. The pills will help you feel better," Noah told her.

"Noah is right." Mercy rose and brought the medicine to the table and handed Anna two pills.

While she didn't like to take medication, with her wrist hurting so badly, she was afraid she wouldn't be able to sleep. Anna swallowed the pills.

"Now, bedtime. Off you go. You need a *gut* night's rest. I will check in on you in a little while."

Anna slowly rose to her feet, leaned in, and kissed Mercy's cheek. "I don't know what I would do without you." She gave her mother-in-law a smile, then headed for the stairs. When she reached the bedroom, she paused for a moment and leaned back against the doorframe. *What must Noah be thinking about his homecoming so far?*

Her precious daughter slept, unaware of the turmoil in her Mamm's heart. Anna struggled to get undressed with only one good hand. Once changed into her nightgown, she slipped under the covers next to Chloe, careful not to wake her.

Chloe was her world. She couldn't imagine her life without this sweet child.

As she waited for sleep, she couldn't help but wonder what the future held for Noah. He seemed thoroughly English now, but his Mamm clearly longed for his return to the Rexford community. Once he left, would any of them be the same?

The Yoders brought back Marta and the buggy just after Anna had gone upstairs. "It's repairable," Carl said. "The horse is inside the barn, but she'll need tending. I can have one of my boys do it." Clearly the man doubted that Noah could handle the job, and who could blame him? Noah had been gone a long time.

Noah shook his head. "We're grateful for your help. But I can manage."

Mercy nodded and said, "Danki, Carl, for all you and your sons have done. May I offer you something to eat and drink?"

"Lydia will be waiting for us. Please let us know if there is more we can do. Good night, Mercy." The Yoders left. Noah wasn't surprised by Carl's attitude. Most Amish had a basic mistrust of anyone in law enforcement and, added to the circumstances under which he'd left the community, Noah couldn't expect much from anyone.

His mother's voice broke the silence. "What happened out there tonight, Noah? Was the wreck an accident?"

Noah didn't need his CIA training to see that his mother's worry went much deeper than Anna's injuries. What Dr. Montgomery had said to him earlier had troubled him since he'd hung up the phone. Could three accidents still be considered as such, or was someone deliberately targeting his family?

"Why would you ask that?" He held his mother's gaze. "Mamm, what happened to Daed?" Without even realizing, Noah reverted to the language of his youth, even though he hadn't spoken more than a handful of words in it these past ten years.

"An *Unfall*, Noah. Only an accident." Mercy shook her head. "Henry was working on the floor in the loft. This past winter was harsh, and the floor has needed replacing for a while. Some boards were warped. While Henry was fixing them, I guess he forgot to nail some of them down. He stepped wrong. He fell through to the ground and—" She stopped speaking as tears spilled from her eyes. "He was barely alive when Dr. Montgomery got here. The doctor and I rode to the hospital with your Daed. He died soon after we got there." She pressed a trembling hand against her mouth.

Noah didn't know what to say. Nothing about what his mother said rang true. His Daed had taken pride in his work and keeping his home and barns in tip-top shape. Nor could he see his father taking unnecessary chances by not nailing boards in place.

"Why was he working up there alone? Why wasn't someone from the community there to help him out?" In the Rexford that he remembered, everyone watched out for one another, as the Yoders had helped tonight. He knew that spirit of cooperation had not changed.

Mercy shook her head. "You know your Daed. He preferred to be the one lending a hand. He would only ask for assistance for himself if he truly needed it." She lifted her shoulders and patted Noah's hand. "But he loved working with his sons more than he could ever say. He always held out hope that one day you would return to the community and join the family again."

Noah felt as if someone had punched him in the stomach. He swallowed hard, but the lump in his throat wouldn't go away. He'd lost so many years with his Daed. Now he was gone for good, and Noah wouldn't get the chance to make up for lost time.

He would never forget that day long ago when he'd told his Daed he was leaving the community. No one but his Daed knew the real reason behind Noah's need to leave so abruptly. Henry Petersheim hadn't tried to discourage his son. He'd simply driven Noah to Eureka and stood tall and strong as he watched his boy board a bus headed for Billings. Henry never once shed a tear in Noah's presence, but Noah had no doubt that his leaving had broken his Daed's heart.

"I'm sorry I wasn't there for him," he whispered hoarsely. Henry deserved better. So did his Mamm.

Mercy clasped her son's hand. "He loved you, Noah. He understood why you left. I know there was more to your leaving than what was told to us, but your Daed never gave your secrets away."

Noah stumbled to his feet. He couldn't bear the thought of how badly he'd hurt his Daed. "I need to tend to Marta."

Mercy didn't try to stop him. He donned his jacket and headed out into the cold night, resisting the urge to keep right on walking back to the car and drive back to Langley. Forget his life here in Rexford forever. But he couldn't. Mamm needed him.

And her description of what had happened to Daed still weighed heavily on his mind.

At the entrance to the barn, something out of place captured his attention. Footsteps in the snow. Multiple ones. The Yoders', of course, and they'd driven off in their own buggy after towing Anna's buggy home. The explanation was simple. So why did he feel so uneasy?

Noah slowly pushed the door open. Darkness greeted him. He switched on the small flashlight he carried in his coat pocket.

"Is anyone in here?" The question was ridiculous. His only answer was the nickering of horses: Marta as well as his Mamm's, Esther and Jenny. He shined his flashlight around the interior, then found and lit a lantern.

Overhead, the rafters of the barn were visible through a gaping hole. *Daed died here. Alone.* Guilt swamped him.

"I'm sorry I wasn't here for you." His voice, only a whisper, nonetheless echoed through the barn.

Noah began brushing Marta down. The snow had soaked through her coat. He found a towel and dried her before placing a blanket over her and leading her to one of the stalls. Once he'd made sure she and the others had plenty of food and water, he shut the stall door. He hadn't cared for horses in years, but the skills came back effortlessly. The work had been soothing. Satisfying. Somehow, he felt his father's approval.

Yet as he thought about returning to the house, he realized he wasn't ready to face his mother again. He should examine the buggy. The Yoders had brought that inside along with the horse. Running his light over the exterior, he could see that, while it was still operable—after all, the Yoders had towed it home—there was plenty of work needed to fix the buggy. He'd do his best for Anna so she'd have safe transportation, and if he couldn't, he'd hire someone to do it right.

The hole in the loft. He took one last look at the buggy. There was nothing he could do tonight, and he couldn't ignore the hole in the loft any longer. Noah brought the lantern to the ladder leading up to the loft and slowly climbed the rungs. Once there, he carefully made his way to the spot where his father had fallen through. Kneeling, he examined the boards. Nothing appeared out of the ordinary, except that the wood floor was in bad shape in this section of the barn. A couple of the boards were warped beyond repair and had rotted through.

But his mother's report didn't add up with what he knew about his father. Henry would never have taken unnecessary risks when working alone. He would have seen the decayed wood and avoided stepping there. He certainly wouldn't have missed securing any boards, as his mother said.

Not that you've been around enough to know for sure. Noah's father might have aged a lot during the time Noah had been gone, and he was simply unable to keep the barn in good repair. And Noah hadn't been there to help.

Noah's thoughts turned to his brother's death. That had been deemed an accident too. The horse he'd been riding had lost his footing while he was on the neighboring property, close to a sheer drop. Joseph must not have had time to react before both he and the horse plunged to their deaths.

One is an accident. Two is strange. Three . . . is something far worse.

Noah went back down the ladder, out the barn door, and into the night. The snow had continued to taper off, but even so the footprints he'd noticed earlier had been partially filled in while he'd been inside the barn. Why was he so fixated on them?

As a CIA agent, he'd had to rely on his instincts more times than he cared to remember, and they rarely failed him. They were pinging like crazy now. He shone the lantern light on the crystalline surface of the ground. There were several sets of tracks, as he'd expected. Carl Yoder had brought two sons with him, and Noah had added his own marks as well.

He took a few steps back to get a broader view, then suddenly he knew. Buggy wheel tracks and prints made by heavy boots were pointed toward the barn door, and also back toward the house, consistent with the paths Noah and the Yoders would have taken. But other tracks led off at an angle, around the side of the barn. Noah could think of no reason why the neighbors would have gone in—or come from—that direction, especially on a night like this. They would have wanted to complete their act of kindness and get back home as quickly as possible.

Dread slipped into the pit of his stomach as he followed the tracks around the barn and partway into the field beyond. He didn't need to go any farther. As far as the small light would allow, he could see that the tracks extended toward the woods in more or less a straight line.

Why would someone come from the woods, to the barn, then go back the same way? And on the same night Anna had been involved in a hit-and-run accident? The coincidence was tough to explain away.

4

She was so cold and someone was coming. Footsteps vibrated on the icy ground. She couldn't move. Had they come to finish her off? She tried to scream but no sound came forth as someone clasped her arm and shook her.

Anna's eyes opened and she stared at the ceiling, her heart racing. Someone was shaking her arm for real. "Mamm!" Chloe's eyes were huge in her face.

"Oh, my *Boppli*. I'm okay. I just had a bad dream." She gathered Chloe close and held her while her daughter cried. How long had she been dreaming? The nightmare had seemed so real that her heart felt ready to explode in her chest.

Daylight filtered through the lace curtains. Someone was hammering loudly. The sound was an unwelcome accompaniment to the pain in Anna's head. "Come, Chloe. It's time to get out of bed before we sleep the day away." She made a funny face to ease the moment, and Chloe giggled.

Anna and Chloe climbed out of bed and donned calf-length, full-skirted dresses. Next came the apron and cape, which Anna secured at the waist with straight pins, moving gingerly because of her injured wrist.

Once her hair was braided—another task that was hampered by her stiff wrist—she wound it on top of her head into a bun before putting on her Kapp. She hadn't done her usual neat job, but she'd done the best she could.

Anna glanced around the simple bedroom that her husband had

once shared with Noah. She felt closer to him, though it had been many years since he had lived here and Mercy had now fitted it up as a guest room, with a full-size bed rather than the two twins that had been here before. A simple wooden dresser had been pushed against the wall closest to the door. A small nightstand sat next to the bed, which was covered in a colorful quilt Anna had made last year as a gift for her mother-in-law.

Once Chloe was dressed for the day, Anna clasped Chloe's hand with her uninjured one. "Let's go find your Grossmammi before we miss breakfast completely." Together they left the bedroom and followed the aroma of food cooking in the kitchen.

Like the bedroom, the rest of the house was simply furnished. The woodstove in the middle of the great room was flanked by a sofa and end table on one side, two comfortable chairs on the other. Mercy had a worn desk that she'd brought with her when she and Henry were married.

"*Ach*, there you two are. You were sleeping so nicely when I checked on you earlier that I didn't have the heart to wake you. You had a difficult night," Mercy said with sympathy and then lifted Chloe up into her arms. "And how is my Boppli today?"

Chloe giggled at the familiar way her Grossmammi referred to her as a baby, even though Anna had done the same thing not ten minutes ago. "I'm not a baby. I'm five in September."

"You will always be my Boppli. Now, come have your breakfast. Anna, would you call Noah in, if you feel able to? He was up early this morning working on the buggy in the barn."

Anna glanced out the kitchen window and froze. In the distance, beyond the barn, someone stood at the edge of the woods. Just as suddenly, the figure was gone. Had she been wrong? Was her head injury causing her to imagine things?

"Anna? Is everything *oke*?" Mercy asked.

Anna gathered her composure and faced her mother-in-law. "I thought I saw someone in the woods. I was mistaken." She smiled reassuringly. "I'll go fetch Noah now."

With her hands trembling, Anna went to the entrance, took her warm woolen cloak and bonnet from the pegs on the wall, then braced for the cold wind that greeted her. The last thing she wanted to do was leave the safety and warmth of the house. But she held the cloak closer to her body and headed for the barn. The hammering stopped and the quiet of the countryside returned.

Anna fought the wind to open the barn door. Once inside, her eyes grew accustomed to the dim light coming from a lantern hanging on the stall door. Noah was nowhere in sight.

"Hello?" she called out. "Noah?"

A noise from above drew her attention up to the loft. Noah's head appeared beside the ladder, his hair ruffled from work. "Good morning! Hang on a second," he called. "I'll be right down."

Since Henry's sudden death, she hated coming in here because of the difficult memories of that day. She missed him terribly.

Up above, she could hear Noah moving around. A few minutes later, he carefully made his way down the ladder. He had pushed up the sleeves of his fleece coat to reveal bare forearms, even though it was cold enough that Anna could see her breath.

As a little girl, she had loved spending time with Noah and her brother. In spite of being several years younger than the boys, she had never felt like an unwelcome intruder on their time. Now, she was a grown woman who knew very little about his life.

"What were you doing up there?" she asked, mostly to fill the empty space.

When he didn't answer right away, she felt terrible. As hard as it was for her, she couldn't imagine how difficult seeing the place where his Daed had fallen to his death must have been for Noah.

"I was securing some boards. How are you feeling this morning?" Noah's searching blue eyes met hers.

Her chest grew tight. She struggled to draw enough air into her lungs.

"I'm feeling much better." She pointed toward the house with her left hand, unsure of why she suddenly felt so nervous around Noah. This was her husband's brother, even though he'd been away a long time. "Your Mamm asked me to come get you. She has breakfast ready."

He nodded and peered up at the loft once more, a solemn expression on his face.

Her heart went out to him. "I'm sorry about your Daed. He was a good man, and I loved him dearly. He is much missed."

Noah's jaw worked with emotion. He seemed to be struggling to find words. "We should probably go inside. Mamm will be waiting, and you should be resting."

Noah held the door open for her, and she unintentionally brushed against him as she passed by, her heart beating a strange rhythm at the brief touch. Anna tucked her gloved hands beneath her cloak for warmth. The cold air stung her cheeks.

A strange, uneasy feeling washed over her. She stopped, then turned to study the nearby woods where she thought she'd spotted someone earlier.

Noah followed her line of sight. "Is something wrong?"

Anna continued to stare toward the trees, yet she saw nothing that shouldn't be there. "I thought I saw something in the woods. I guess I'm still a little shaken up over what happened last night."

Worry creased his forehead. "Last night when I put Marta away, I noticed footprints leading off into the woods."

Anna remembered something her father-in-law told her once. "Henry always allowed hunters to use the barn whenever they needed somewhere to warm up. Maybe the footprints were left by one of them." Henry extended a helping hand to anyone in need. He lived his faith.

"That was Daed. He never met a stranger," Noah said, his voice rough with emotion. "It isn't hunting season. But there's probably a simple explanation." He was clearly trying to be reassuring. So why did she still feel uneasy?

They started walking again. Changing the subject seemed like a good idea. "Your Mamm is so happy to have you home."

"I know she is." The muscle still worked in his jaw. "I wish I could stay longer, but that's not possible. I hope she understands that my life isn't in Rexford anymore."

Anna clutched his arm, stopping him. "You'll stay for a while, won't you? She needs you, Noah. More than she will ever say."

When he didn't answer, she withdrew her hand. The man beside her was a stranger. She shouldn't have suggested he stay. He'd been gone too long. He was English now.

They reached the house and Noah opened the door and waited for her to go in. The icy look in his eyes told her he hadn't liked what she'd said about his mother. He was struggling with being home again, and she'd just made it worse.

Anna slipped past him and went inside. Taking off her cloak, she hung the garment on one of the pegs. Noah was no longer a carefree boy. He and Joseph had been close, and she understood only too well how hard Joseph's death had been. But there was no escaping the fact that until some decisions and plans were made, Noah's family needed him right now.

In the kitchen, Chloe and Mercy were giggling. She followed the sound, knowing Noah would follow.

"There you two are!" Mercy exclaimed when she caught sight of them. She pointed to the table. "Sit, please."

Anna loved the sound of her daughter's laughter. There had been little reason for merriment lately. "Have you two been having fun?" she asked.

Chloe nodded happily. The child's resilience after all the things she'd gone through amazed her.

Mercy had barely set a plate of brown sugar-and-oatmeal pancakes in front of Chloe before she snatched a bite. "Prayers first," Mercy gently chided.

They all bowed their heads and prayed silently. Once the prayer ended, Chloe dug into the treat with eagerness and Noah chuckled at the child's enthusiasm.

"Brown sugar pancakes are my favorite too," he said, winking.

Chloe's eyes grew wide. "They are?"

He nodded and snuck a piece of her pancake.

She giggled and stole a bite of his.

Anna was pleased that Chloe had taken to Noah so easily, and he to her. She'd seen him only a handful of times, and she probably didn't remember all of them, since she was so young. His presence was good for both Chloe and Mercy. And for Anna herself, though she couldn't have said why.

He chose that moment to glance her way, and Anna dragged in an unsteady breath. She just wasn't used to being around him yet.

"You spoil her, Mercy." Anna speared a piece of pancake and savored the bite. No one made pancakes like her mother-in-law.

The older woman beamed, her eyes regaining their old sparkle. "Nonsense. That is a Grossmammi's job, isn't it?"

Anna chuckled at the typical Mercy answer. Family was everything to the Amish and to Anna. She was grateful for all the years she'd had with Henry as her father-in-law. Their quiet talks were one of many things she would miss. The past year without Joseph would have been impossible to get through without him. Now she and Mercy leaned on each other to get through losing Henry as well.

Anna caught Mercy watching her with a sad smile on her face. "*Vee bisht doo?* Are you feeling okay?"

"*Ja*, very well." Yet nothing could have been further from the truth. Her head pounded like someone was banging against her skull. Her wrist ached as well. But she was alive. Everything else was minor.

Still, she couldn't help but think about all the things she needed to do. With the sprained wrist, she wouldn't be able to fulfill her housekeeping duties for days at the very least. She would have to find a way to let the Lathams know that she couldn't come to work for a while.

Mercy patted her hand. "Don't worry so much, Anna. Gött will provide. He always has."

Anna forced a smile for Mercy's sake. "Yes, He does." She hesitated for a second, hating to bring up the difficult subject again. "Now that Noah is home, you will need the extra room. Chloe and I should return to our house."

Tears brimmed in Mercy's eyes, but she nodded. "I know. Still, I wish you didn't have to. I will miss you both so much. Especially this one's bright smile." She touched Chloe's cheek affectionately. "But you and Chloe are only a brisk walk away, and I can use the exercise." She patted her stomach.

Anna clasped her hand. "And we will visit every day. Don't worry. You will tire of us soon enough."

Mercy shook her head. "That would be impossible. Eat your food, Anna. You need to regain your strength. Noah, will you take Anna home to get her quilt and wall hangings for the bulk foods store? Chloe can stay here with me until you both return."

Anna's breath caught when Noah's gaze found hers again.

"Of course," he said, a hint of his familiar grin playing about his mouth. "Anna, I hope you saw the way she managed to get extra time with this one." He pointed to Chloe.

Anna couldn't help but laugh. "I did." She let go of the breath she'd been holding in. She couldn't remember the last time she'd felt this way. "Are you sure you don't mind the trip into town? This is your first full day home."

He shook his head, and the grin became a full-blown smile. She'd forgotten how handsome he was when he smiled. As a child, she'd been sweet on Noah before he left town and she and Joseph began courting.

"I'm sure. I haven't visited the town in years. I'm looking forward to seeing the shops again."

His blue eyes seemed to pierce her, and suddenly she was uncomfortable beneath his gaze. "That's very kind of you." Anna carried her and Chloe's dishes to the sink and turned on the tap, needing to put space between them. Clearly she was still feeling the effects of the accident because her thoughts and feelings were jumbled.

Noah followed her to the sink. "How do you plan to wash dishes with that wrist? Let me do them."

"Nonsense," Mercy interrupted. "Leave them for me. Chloe and I will make short work of this chore."

Anna gave in. Getting her wares to the store was more important than dishes. She bent to give Chloe a kiss. "Don't tire your Grossmammi out too much today."

"Don't worry about me." Mercy was quick to reassure. "Chloe and I know how to watch out for each other, don't we, love?" She took the child's hand. "You take care of your business. We will be fine on our own."

"I'll get Daed's buggy ready and meet you outside." Noah headed out the door.

She was impressed that he seemed to understand that even though his fancy car would be warmer and make quicker work of the trip, she would still be more comfortable in a buggy. Cars were only for emergencies or very long journeys.

Chloe had already begun tugging at Mercy's hand. Anna knew exactly what she wanted.

"Let's go outside and play in the snow, Grossmammi."

Building snow angels and playing in the snow was one of Chloe's favorite things to do lately, and she could be relentless at times.

Anna started to tell her no, but Mercy stopped her.

"Leave her be. I enjoy pretending to be a child again from time to time."

Sadness filled Mercy's voice, and Anna forgot all about her protests. She went to her mother-in-law and hugged her close as the woman struggled to contain her grief.

"I know you miss them. I do too. And you're right. Playing in the snow can be fun."

Mercy brushed aside tears and gave Anna a sad smile. "Ja." She touched Anna's arm, her smile disappearing. "I wish he could stay this time. For good."

Anna struggled to keep her answer positive. From what she'd witnessed so far, Noah had no intention of sticking around for long. She chose her words carefully. "Having Noah here is good for you."

"And for you and Chloe as well. She could use a good male role model in her life now that Henry . . ." Her voice broke when she struggled to speak again. "We need Noah here with us, Anna. Not out there in the dangerous world he lives in."

Anna turned away before Mercy could see her reaction. As much as she prayed Noah was home to stay for Mercy's sake, she knew it wasn't true. He'd left the plain ways behind long ago, choosing the English world instead. It wouldn't be long before he grew tired of their simple way of life and moved on. And when that happened, she couldn't imagine how hard that would be for Mercy and Chloe.

And, she had to admit, for herself.

Anna emerged from the house, tugging her cloak closer to her body, her petite frame hunched against the biting wind. Noah's protective instincts were close to the surface. She was good and sweet, and she didn't deserve any of the things that she'd had to go through in the last year.

He held out his hand. She clasped it with her good hand, then hoisted herself up to the buggy's bench next to him. Noah waited until she was settled before grabbing the thick blanket he'd brought from the house and placing the cover over her lap.

She smiled in gratitude, then he urged the mare down the well-worn path to Anna's home. She was unusually quiet, and he sensed something troubled her.

"I hope you don't mind taking me to Mrs. Schwartz's Bulk Foods Store today. Your mother can be very . . . persuasive at times."

"She can be at that, but I don't mind at all. To tell the truth, I'm not sure what I'm supposed to be doing now that I am home. Planting season is still a few weeks away." He shrugged.

Sympathy pooled in her eyes. "I can't imagine how difficult this must be for you to come back to a different way of life, unsure where your place is any longer." She placed a gloved hand on his arm. "Give it time. You will figure things out, I'm positive."

He wasn't nearly as convinced. Not that it mattered. "I'm not sure I am going to be here that long."

"Mercy is happy to have you home for however long you plan to stay."

"And you? Are you happy I'm home?" As soon as the question was out, he regretted it. What had made him ask such a thing? Now he'd made her uncomfortable.

"Of course. And so is Chloe," she said evenly.

She'd brought the conversation back to safer ground, giving him a reprieve he wasn't sure he deserved.

"She's a wonderful girl. You've done a great job with her."

Anna swallowed visibly. "She misses her Daed so much. And Henry was wonderful with her."

She stopped, but he could read her next thoughts as easily as if she'd said them aloud. With Henry gone, Chloe's life would be missing an important influence. He'd give anything to be able to fill the void for Chloe. But it wasn't his place. Soon he'd be leaving.

"Daed had a special way with kids. He was patient and gentle, just a big kid himself when he wanted to be."

Noah's thoughts drifted back to the gaping hole in the loft floor. Seeing it in the light of day had solidified his belief that his father would never have deliberately put himself in jeopardy, as was obvious from the accident scene. Something else must have happened. But what?

He became aware of her watching him, and he shoved away the image of the broken floorboards. "Have you remembered anything further about the accident last night?"

As soon as his question was out, he felt her tense up. "Anna?" he prompted.

She shook her head. "I only remember what I told you before." She let out a breath. "I don't want to believe someone would have deliberately run me off the road, yet I'm positive the driver must have known he'd hit me. Why would someone do such a thing? Maybe the driver was a traveler, not used to sharing the road with a buggy?" She sounded unconvinced.

Noah wasn't convinced either. He kept recalling the unusual circumstances of his brother's death. All the unanswered questions he'd had back then that were now magnified in light of his father's death and the accident last night. But until he had proof there was something more sinister going on here, he'd keep his doubts to himself. There was no need to alarm anyone.

Noah reined Marta to a stop in front of the house and jumped down. Anna's hand felt so small in his as he helped her down. She had been through so much with her parents' deaths, her husband's, and her father-in-law's. He hated thinking about how hard she worked to get by, and now she was injured.

Her sparkling eyes took his breath away up close. The cold had whipped a lovely pink into her cheeks. She was beautiful. He shook off feelings that had no place in his life. Best not to go there.

"How are you really doing?" he asked when the silence between them became awkward.

She stared out at the breathtaking mountains beyond her place. "I'm *gut*—well, I'm doing the best I can." The truth of that statement was reflected in her forlorn expression.

"I know it's been hard without Joseph," he said before he lost his nerve. "I'm sorry I wasn't here for you."

"You shouldn't feel bad. You have your own life. I wouldn't expect you to change that." She lifted her chin, taking his breath away with the amazing amount of strength she possessed. "But I want to ask you something, and I need you to be honest with me."

Noah dreaded the question he'd been expecting since he'd arrived the night before.

"How long will you stay?" She didn't hesitate to voice the direct question. "Because if you can't stay for a while, you should not let Mercy believe you will. She's convinced this time will be different, and you are home for good."

The fierce protectiveness she showed for his Mamm spoke of the love Anna had for her. She didn't want Mercy to be hurt when he left again. He understood. But he couldn't make promises he wouldn't be able to keep.

Anna was being honest with him. He owed her the same. "I don't know," he admitted. "I love my Mamm very much, but I don't belong here anymore. I'm an outsider now."

She was quick to deny his response. "You are not an outsider. You're family. Rexford can be your home again, if that's what you want. You have to believe that for yourself."

To this he had no answer, and she must have sensed it. She spun around and went up the steps to her house. After a much-needed moment to regain his composure, Noah followed her inside.

"I'll just be a moment. I have the one quilt that's ready and the other things in my room." Her tone was cool.

He waited inside the door without answering. Her honesty had shaken him. Of course, Noah knew his mother wanted him to return to his Amish roots, to settle into being a farmer once more, to marry and have a family of his own. The Amish way. But Mercy didn't know the dark things in his heart. For him, none of those things were possible.

Anna returned a few minutes later carrying a folded quilt and two smaller items, which he thought must be the wall hangings. Noah took the items from her. They were heavier than expected, and he realized that the quilt must be very large.

"May I see the quilt?" When she nodded, he set the wall hangings aside and opened the quilt, laying it out over the bench in the sitting room. "This is lovely, Anna. I can't imagine how much time went into completing it."

The exquisite piece depicted beautiful songbirds flying and sitting on a branch, each bird made up of different patches of cloth against a pale-blue background. Anna had designed the quilt to appear as if the viewer was looking through a window at an outside world filled with birds.

She beamed at his compliment and touched the quilt lovingly. "Making this one, the unfinished one upstairs, and these nine-patch wall hangings helped me get through the long winter."

The reminder of all that she had lost tore at his heart. If he had stayed and faced the truth, would everything have turned out differently? Would both Joseph and his father still be alive?

5

Anna was pleased that Noah appreciated the hard work she'd put into her quilts and wall hangings. She had learned the craft from the women in her community, as had generations before her. She and her childhood friend, Jessie Troyer, had spent many a winter's night together, each working on their separate quilts. In the beginning, they'd dreamed of what their lives would be like once they were married and had families of their own.

Jessie had married the year after Anna and Joseph. She and her *Mann*, Lemuel, were blessed with five girls. The middle daughter was the same age as Chloe, and the two loved to spend time together.

While Anna and Jessie worked on their quilting, all the girls would play. Having a houseful of young ones around to brighten the day was nice.

If only she'd been able to complete the current quilt in time to bring along now, but it couldn't be helped. She prayed all the items would sell quickly. This winter had been a harsh one. There had been many days when she couldn't make it to the Lathams' to work, so money was tight. Now, with Henry gone, she and Mercy desperately needed the money she made cleaning the Lathams' home as well as selling her quilts and wall hangings to get them through spring. Once the garden came in, Mercy would sell her vegetables and fruits on a roadside stand near town, but that was months away.

Would Noah still be here when it came time to plant the spring wheat? If not, then she and Mercy would need to find some able-bodied men to help plow the fields and plant the crop if they were to stand a chance at keeping the farm.

"*Voss iss lets*, Anna?" Noah spoke so softly that at first, she almost didn't catch his use of the language. She only hoped that every emotion she'd just gone through wasn't written plainly on her face.

Anna squared her shoulders and met his gaze. "Nothing is wrong."

"That's not the truth. You have a very expressive face."

She closed her eyes briefly and turned away. Her burdens were her own. She'd get through them with Gött's help like she always had. "I'm just worried about your Mamm. She misses Henry terribly. I hear her crying at night when she thinks I'm sleeping." Anna stopped and shook her head. "I wish there was more that I could do for her."

He clasped her uninjured hand in his, his touch tingling against her skin. "You are doing plenty for her just by being there. She needs that."

She needs you to stay was on the tip of her tongue, but she stopped the words. Saying such a thing was not her place. She'd been out of line when she'd said it earlier. Noah needed to make up his own mind about his future, whether it was here in Rexford or somewhere else.

He refolded the quilt and carried it and the wall hangings outside to the buggy. With one final glance around her home to make sure all was in order, Anna followed him outside.

As they headed toward town, she found herself wondering about Noah's life in the outside world. Mercy had told her he often traveled to other countries.

"You're awfully quiet." Noah slid a sideways look her way, bringing her out of her musings. "What's on your mind?"

"You are, actually," she said with a slight smile. "Your Mamm has shared some things about your life. Are you happy being a spy?"

Anna could tell her question surprised him. He finally shrugged. "I suppose so. As happy as any of us are." While he returned her smile, there was no joy in his eyes. She suspected his answer wasn't completely truthful.

"The type of work you do is hard. Your life is in danger all the time. Do you ever miss the simple ways?" Would he answer her honestly?

"I suppose at times, but I'm good at what I do. I'm happy." His attention returned to the road in front of them, but tension worked in his jaw. Noah obviously didn't like talking about his job. Was it because secrecy was important, or because the work he did wasn't as fulfilling as he wanted her to believe?

Anna decided to keep her questions to herself, and they made the rest of the trip to town in silence.

He steered Marta down the familiar main street. More accumulation had fallen during the night, yet Marta's footing was sure on the snow-covered road.

Even though it was still early, many of the stores were open. The scent of fresh-baked pastries called out to her from Beiler's Bakery. Her Daed would bring her into town when she was a child, and they'd always stop for cinnamon rolls. Everything about this place spoke of home to her. She could not imagine living anywhere else. She loved her community and the people who lived there so much. How did Noah do it?

"Whoa, Marta." Noah brought the mare to a halt in front of Mrs. Schwartz's Bulk Foods Store and hopped down. This time, instead of taking her hand, he grasped her waist and lifted her down and away from the buggy.

She landed much too close to him. Their eyes held, and her chest grew tight.

This is wrong.

So why didn't it feel wrong?

He pointed to the ground. A large amount of ice had formed

beneath the overhang, where she would have stepped. "It's slippery here. I didn't want you to fall." His voice was slightly husky.

Noah let her go and took the bundle, then reached for her hand. "Mind your step. There's a lot of ice here."

He was being helpful, but his touch awakened feelings inside of her that were not welcome. She was his brother's widow.

Noah held the door open for her, and Anna entered the warmth of the building. Though there were only four aisles, the store was crammed with flour, beans, sugar, grains, and meats and cheeses in the coolers. A few years back, Mrs. Schwartz had even made room for a limited amount of Amish clothing and shoes.

As always, Mrs. Schwartz was busy at work even at this early hour. She raised her head and smiled at the sound of the bell above the door.

"Anna." Her smile faded when she spotted Anna's bandaged wrist. "*Voss iss lets mit deekk?*"

Anna did her best to explain the accident without mentioning her unsettling assumptions.

"This is a terrible thing. You poor child." Mrs. Schwartz shook her head in disbelief. "Edward will hate to lose you for any length of time. I know how much he appreciates your hard work."

Anna inclined her head. "I hope I can get back there soon."

Mrs. Schwartz smiled sympathetically. "Ja, but you have to do what is best for you first." She glanced at Noah, but didn't appear to recognize him. She raised a questioning eyebrow at Anna.

"You remember Noah Petersheim, Joseph's brother?"

Noah placed the items on the counter in front of him and held out his hand.

Mrs. Schwartz's expression cleared, and she shook his hand politely and greeted him as she would any Englischer, reminding Anna of what Noah had said earlier about being an outsider now.

"Oh yes. Now I remember. I was sorry to hear about your father. Mercy must be happy to have you home, though."

Noah gave a small nod. "Danki."

Mrs. Schwartz focused on Anna's handiwork. "Well, now, you have brought me some more of your lovely work today, I see." She admired the quilt first.

"Ja. I hope they do as well as the others." She cast a worried glance at Mrs. Schwartz.

The elder woman was quick to reassure her. "I'm sure they will." Mrs. Schwartz understood only too well how difficult things were for her. After her husband's passing a few years back, Mrs. Schwartz had confided that she feared the business wouldn't be able to go on without him.

"I'll take a look around while you two talk." Noah made his way to some of the few men's clothing articles.

"This is lovely, Anna. One of your best. Songbirds are a favorite amongst the English women."

Making the quilt had been part of the healing process for her. She had put her heart and soul—as well as countless tears—into making the quilt. "That's very kind of you to say."

"And the wall hangings are beautiful as well. I'm positive they'll sell quickly. In fact, I will put them right up front in the window display so that everyone who passes by can see them."

Anna swallowed past a sudden lump in her throat, grateful to the kindhearted woman. "You are too good to me."

Mrs. Schwartz brushed off her compliment with a wave of the hand. Then she carried the quilt and wall hangings to her large window and arranged them in an eye-catching display.

Noah appeared next to her. He held a pair of black broadfall pants, a vest, and a simple blue shirt in one hand and a black felt hat in the other. "I think while I'm here I should show respect for my Daed," he explained.

Her heart was full as she smiled up at him. "I think he would appreciate the gesture," she said.

After Mrs. Schwartz rang up Noah's purchases, he thanked her and tucked the bag under his arm.

"We should be on our way. My Chloe is waiting for me at Mercy's," Anna explained. "By now, she's probably had her Grossmammi make at least a dozen snow angels." She waved to Mrs. Schwartz, and then she and Noah headed for the door.

"Take care of yourself, Anna. No more accidents," Mrs. Schwartz called after her as they left the store.

As they stepped outside, Anna glanced up at the cloudless day, and her spirits lifted. Today was one of those rare times when the skies were clear and the air crisp. Who couldn't be happy on a day such as today?

She began to pick her way back to the buggy but Noah stopped her.

"Do you feel like being a little *veesht*?" he asked with a grin on his face.

Anna could feel the color rising in her cheeks. "Bad? What do you mean?"

He pointed behind her at the bakery. "As I recall, you used to love cinnamon rolls. Do you still?"

She couldn't keep from smiling in return. "I do, and I would love one."

"Wait here. I'll put these away." Noah carried his purchases to the buggy and laid them on the seat. Then he came back to her, and they walked side by side to the bakery.

The moment Anna stepped through the door, she stopped. The smell of freshly baked fry pies mingling with that of cinnamon rolls was a delight to her senses. Noah chuckled next to her, and she joined in. She was acting silly, but for some reason she felt happier than she had in a while, despite the pain in her wrist.

"Come on. We'll buy one for Chloe and Mamm as well."

They went up to the counter together where Mrs. Beiler was ready and waiting for them.

"Anna, I heard about the accident." She made a clicking sound with her tongue. "Such a terrible thing. How are you feeling today?"

"I am *gut*. No harm done. Just a few bruises and this." She held up her sprained wrist.

Mrs. Beiler eyed her injury. "I am glad to hear this. The accident could have been far worse."

"Yes. I am grateful to Gött." Anna turned to the man at her side. "You remember Noah, Joseph's brother?"

The woman sized Noah up for the longest time before she answered. "I do. What can I get you both this fine morning?" A hint of frost touched the woman's voice, and Anna's heart went out to Noah. How hard it must be for him to feel like a stranger amongst the people he once called family.

"Four cinnamon rolls, please." Noah ordered in a clipped tone. His jaw tightened. He clearly hadn't missed the disapproving signals the bakery owner was sending.

Mrs. Beiler brought four saucer-sized cinnamon rolls out of the display case and carefully put them in a paper bag, separating them with sheets of waxed paper. She handed Noah the rolls and rang up their order.

They returned to the buggy without saying a word. Anna could tell that the reaction he'd received stung.

"Give them time. You've been away for a while. They'll accept you back again—you'll see."

His smile was forced. "Will they? I never joined the church. As far as they're concerned, I don't belong here."

She wished she could think of something encouraging to say, but he was right.

Once he'd urged Marta down the road, Anna handed him one of the cinnamon rolls. Noah bit into the roll and closed his eyes briefly. "They are as good as I remember. And still warm." He was smiling again. The gloom had passed.

Anna laughed at the joy on his face. "Yes, they are. Some things will never change."

He grinned and brushed a crumb from her mouth. She froze at the touch of his hand against her skin. What was wrong with her? Why couldn't she relax around him?

She took another bite and stared at the road in front of them.

"Would you mind if I stopped by the community phone?" she asked, hoping she sounded normal. "I need to call Mr. and Mrs. Latham and let them know I won't be coming in for a while."

He shook his head. "No, of course not." Noah steered Marta toward the phone shanty nearby.

Anna remembered the things Edward had said to her before she left his home the day before—how long ago it seemed. His words had been both frightening and timely, almost as if Gött had been trying to warn her through the kind man.

Noah stopped the mare next to the shanty and hopped down. She did the same before he could come around the buggy and help her, recalling the touch of his hands around her waist earlier. Her own reaction had shocked her, and she vowed not to allow herself to be in that position again.

He was a good and honorable man. She believed that if he chose to stay, he would be welcomed back into the community in time. Why would he want to live a life of solitude in the English world? If he did. She really had no idea what his life outside of Rexford was like.

While she waited for the call to go through, she found herself glancing around. She couldn't shake the feeling that someone was watching her, much like she'd felt at the barn. Yet very few people were about at this early hour. Was this a consequence of the bump she'd suffered to her head? How long would it take before the repercussions of last night faded? Anna lifted up a prayer to Gött to strengthen her faith.

Noah stood close to Marta, rubbing the mare's nose and peering around the area as if looking for trouble. Did he sense something too?

"Hello?" The familiar voice of her employer brought her back to the moment.

"Hello, Edward, its Anna."

"Anna, how are you? Is everything okay?" Calling her employer was unusual for her, so naturally, he was worried.

She drew in a breath and did her best to explain about the accident without alarming him.

"Oh my goodness, Anna, I'm so sorry to hear that. I can't believe such a thing would happen here in this peaceful community. Do you need anything? Anything at all?"

Anna was left with the impression that Edward wasn't surprised by the news of her accident. But then again, the people living in the area surrounding the Rexford community, both English and Amish, were a close-knit group. News traveled fast.

"That's very kind of you, but I'm fine. I wanted to let you know that I won't be coming to work for a couple of weeks. Dr. Montgomery wants me to rest my wrist. But as soon as I'm able, I will be back. I hope this doesn't inconvenience you too much."

Edward was quick to reassure her. "Absolutely not. Don't worry about us. We will be ready for you to return to work whenever you are able. Don't hesitate to call again if you need anything at all."

"Thank you." She hung up the phone, relieved he'd been so supportive. But two weeks was a long time to be without her normal income. Her mind struggled to come up with something to help fill in the gap. She had some older quilts she had made a few years back. If she could talk Mrs. Schwartz into displaying them, the extra money that would come if they sold would go a long way in helping her and Mercy get through the next two weeks.

Once they were on their way home again, Anna did her best to put her worries aside. "Chloe will be so pleased with her treat." She held up the bag. "She loves cinnamon rolls almost as much as I do."

"I'm not surprised. She's a great girl. This past year could not have been easy for either of you."

She looked out across the snowy fields. "I feel terrible for Chloe. She misses her father so much." Tears misted her eyes as she recalled wonderful memories of the three of them together.

Noah said nothing, as if waiting for her to continue by herself.

"He used to come home from working the field until dark, and then he and Chloe would play together, no matter how tired he was." Her voice shook as she recalled the special relationship her Mann had shared with their little girl. "He loved taking her ice-skating. Going to Emerson's Pond was one of their favorite things to do together. I'm no good at it, and with Henry being so busy, I'm afraid she missed out this year."

Something came and went in Noah's eyes. Was he remembering her brother's tragic accident while ice-skating? Of course he was. How thoughtless of her to bring it up.

She still recalled the first time Chloe had asked to go skating. One of Jessie's daughters had told her about the pond and Chloe had begged her Daed to take her. Joseph had bravely put his daughter's happiness above his own and taken Chloe skating. The outing had turned out to be a joyous time, and Anna suspected it had helped her Mann heal from at least some of his pain. Joseph was a strong man, and she was lucky to have shared her life with him.

When he'd first come to her and confessed the dark secret he'd held on to since Adam's death, Anna had been surprised. Joseph had been unable live with what had happened any longer. He'd insisted on speaking with Bishop Eicher and the elders of the church. He'd carried the burden far too long. Joseph had accepted his punishment without trying to plead his case. Then he'd worked hard to regain his place in the community, and the shunning had been removed shortly before his death.

A wintry smile touched Noah's lips. "Joseph and I used to go there all the time when we were kids. We both loved skating." He shifted uncomfortably. "Maybe I could take her someday soon. There should still be plenty of good ice out there."

His generous offer amazed her. "That's kind, Noah, but you don't have to. I know how hard it would be for you."

The pain was visible in his eyes. "Joseph would want me to be there for Chloe, and I want to as well." The muscle worked in his jaw. "I can't say it will be easy. I haven't been skating since that time, but I will try for Chloe's sake. She's my niece, and I love her. I want to get to know her."

Anna could only nod. As happy as she was that Noah wanted to spend time with her daughter, she was worried that when the time came for him to leave, Chloe would feel the loss of another family member deeply.

"She will be so happy," she said, instead of voicing her worries aloud. "I'm pretty sure I still have Joseph's old skates, and they should fit you. After you've had a chance to settle in, we can plan a trip there. I can make us a picnic." She got caught up in the excitement of the prospect.

He smiled at her enthusiasm. "That sounds nice, but you will be skating too, right?"

"After what happened to Adam ..." She didn't finish, immediately feeling like a coward. She hadn't skated since that day, but she'd thought he could?

But there was no reproach in his voice when he spoke. "Since being back on the ice will be hard for both of us, maybe we can help each other. We'll go slow. I know Chloe would love you to join us." He clasped her hand. "We'll get through it together."

She really wanted to. Chloe deserved something fun in her life. Anna tried to convince herself she was going for her daughter's sake, yet she was strangely looking forward to the outing as well. Could she finally face the loss of her brother after all these years?

Adam had spent every moment of his tragically short life living it to the fullest, much like his friend Joseph. She could almost hear them scolding her. *Stop living in the past, Anna. We're okay, and what happened is over and done with. Chloe needs you to move forward for her. Start living again.*

The thought of moving on without them hurt, but she had no choice. She had to do what was best for Chloe.

"Okay, but you have to promise not to let me fall."

He stopped and gazed solemnly at her. "I promise. I'll never let you fall again."

Noah held up the bag from Beiler's Bakery as they walked into the house. When Chloe spotted it, her eyes lit up, and she ran to cling to his legs. She was such a happy and affectionate child. After the things she'd gone through, her joy surprised and delighted him. Spending time with her reminded him of the things lacking in his life.

He scooped her up and handed her the bag. "There's one there for your Grossmammi too."

Chloe opened the bag. "Cinnamon rolls!" she squealed as if he'd given her the greatest gift ever. Then she hugged him tight. "Danki, *Onkel* Noah."

Hearing the little girl call him *uncle* for the first time swelled his heart. He ruffled her hair and then set her back down. "You are welcome, Kind."

Noah's glance slid to Anna standing next to him. He'd enjoyed being with her this morning. He couldn't remember the last time he'd enjoyed much of anything.

"I should go pack up our things," she told her child. "Enjoy your cinnamon roll with your Grossmammi, and then we must be on our way. I'm sure Noah has things he would like to do today, such as getting settled into his old room." With a quick look his way, Anna went upstairs, and he found himself watching her far longer than he should have.

She believed he could come home to Rexford for good. She said he could fit back into the community as if he'd always been here, but she didn't know the truth. Would she hate him when she did?

"Shall we enjoy these wonderful cinnamon rolls together, Chloe?" Mercy put the rolls on a plate and brought out some fresh milk.

Noah shook off his guilt with difficulty and sat at the table next to them. The past was best left where it was. The damage was done. He couldn't rewrite history.

Chloe took a huge bite of the roll, which left icing on her nose. She giggled. In so many ways, she reminded him of himself and Joseph when they were that age, full of enthusiasm for life. Each day had brought a new adventure. If only they had known what the future held back then, he would have done so many things differently.

His thoughts drifted back to his brother's accident. Horses got spooked for sure. Accidents happened as part of the Amish way of life, but now his father was dead too.

"Was anything unusual happening in Daed's life lately?" he asked his mother, then peeked over at Chloe to make sure the child wasn't paying attention to the adults' conversation.

Mercy's brows knitted together. Of course she wouldn't see her husband's death as anything suspicious. Mercy only saw the good in people and wouldn't suspect anyone of wanting to harm her husband or son. But the accidents were stacking up, and his instincts told him something was wrong.

"Why would you ask such a thing? There's been nothing different about your Daed's life in years. He worked hard to keep the farm going. He was a good man."

Noah tried to soften his questions. His mother was still grieving her husband's death. He didn't want to push too hard. "I meant did he have dealings with anyone new? Was he having trouble with someone that he might have mentioned to you?"

Mercy squared her shoulders, pinning him with a stern gaze. "Noah Petersheim, your Daed did not have trouble. He lived a simple life. A humble life. Trouble wasn't part of his world."

Noah realized if he was going to get any real answers, they wouldn't come from his mother. "You're right. I'm sorry I brought it up."

Chloe finished her cinnamon roll and held up her sticky fingers for them to see. "I'm a mess, Grossmammi," she said proudly.

"I see that. Go wash up," Mercy told the child. "It's almost time for you and your Mamm to go."

When it was the two of them again, Noah placed his hand over hers. "I didn't mean to upset you."

Tears brimmed in her eyes. Another reason for regret. He had so many. "I'm oke," she said with a sigh. "I just miss him terribly. Not a day goes by that I don't wish for one more moment with him."

Noah couldn't imagine how hard it must be for her. He bowed his head. "I know. I feel the same way. And I wish I could do something to make things better for you."

"You could. Stay. This is where you belong, Noah. It's what your Daed wanted."

The wealth of hurt those words brought stuck in his throat.

"I can't," he said as gently as he could, wishing he could make her understand. The disappointment on her face sent a pang through his heart. "I will stay as long as possible and do what I can to help with the farm, so don't worry. Before I leave, I will hire some of the local men to help with the spring planting. Everything will be okay, I promise. I'm sorry, but my life is no longer here. I'm not Amish anymore, and I have a job waiting for me back home."

The tears in her eyes assured him this was not the answer she had hoped for. "All right, Soh." The weariness in her voice tore at his heart. "You must do what is best for you. Ask Gött to direct your path."

He couldn't tell her that he wasn't sure Gött listened to his prayers anymore. Gött knew the secrets of his heart, and they weren't good.

Before he could think of an answer, Anna came into the room carrying a bag, and Noah rose to his feet. "Ready?" he asked, almost relieved for the interruption.

He'd hurt his mother by his answer. She wanted things that he couldn't give her. As much as he wished he could stay, it was impossible. This world was no longer his.

Anna's eyes darted from his Mamm to him as if she knew what had been said.

"I am ready. Chloe, give your Grossmammi a kiss before we leave."

Chloe rushed to Mercy and wrapped little arms around her waist. His mother picked her up and held the child tight. This was an emotional time for her. He hated that he'd added to her pain.

"I've gotten so used to having you here, my Boppli. I will miss seeing both your smiling faces each morning." Mercy wiped tears away with her apron.

Anna went over and gave Mercy a hug as well. "You know we will stop by each day to see you, and Chloe can spend the night whenever you like."

A smile brightened Mercy's face. "That would be lovely. Danki, Anna."

Anna kissed her cheek. "Of course. We're family. We take care of each other."

Mercy clutched her hand. "We do."

With one final hug, Anna and Chloe headed for the door.

Noah took the bag Anna held and opened the door for them. Before he left, he turned back for another glimpse of his mother. She sat staring sadly at the fire through the glass door of the woodstove. Her hurt was his. She had lost so much and wanted him to return to the Amish way of life, but Mercy didn't know the depths of despair every inch of this place held for him. The guilt he experienced every single time he returned to Rexford. He knew he wouldn't be able to stand the shunning Joseph had endured. His younger brother had always been stronger than he. If the truth were to be discovered now, he would not be welcome here, and he had no doubt that his Mamm—and Anna—would hate him.

He would give anything to be the man these women needed him

to be. Could he ever return to his Amish roots again? Could he live with the pain he'd caused? He didn't see how.

Noah waved goodbye and then joined Anna and Chloe, who waited for him in the buggy. If he were being honest with himself, every time he looked at Anna he felt the same guilt. She had loved Joseph with all her heart and married him. She'd stood by him during his shunning, which couldn't have been easy.

He hopped up onto the seat next to Chloe, aware of Anna's watchful eyes on him.

"Is something wrong?" she asked softly, concern written on her face.

Could he tell her the truth? His heart wanted to be free of the ugly secret that held him frozen in time, but he was afraid. There was too much to lose. And he was a coward.

He shook his head. It was the only answer he could give right now. With Chloe tucked between him and Anna, preventing her from asking any specific questions, Noah urged the mare down the path between his family home and Anna's.

He still felt bad about uprooting Anna and his niece. His mother enjoyed having them there so much. She needed them with her more than she needed him there.

"Are you sure you and Chloe don't want to stay with my Mamm instead? I could move into your home for a while."

Anna wouldn't hear of it. "Don't be silly, Noah. Your Mamm needs you with her now. She's a strong woman, but she's struggling with Henry's death. I'm glad you're home, for however long you can stay."

He wished he felt the same way. Rexford was the last place he wanted to be, yet somehow the only place he longed to be. Everything about his former home reminded him of his childhood foolishness—the lies he'd told, the choices he'd made. Joseph had idolized his older brother and Noah didn't deserve that honor.

"Being back here must be hard." Anna had seen something in his expression and knew he needed to talk, in spite of what he'd said.

"Yes," he managed. "I missed so much time with my Daed. I'd give anything to have a little more of his wisdom. His kindness. His strength." He swallowed back his regret. No matter what he wished, he couldn't turn back time. He'd failed his father miserably. Now, when he left again, he'd do the same to his mother.

When he'd first learned of his father's death, he'd told his commander that he needed to take an extended leave of absence. Only his superiors at the agency knew about his life here in Montana. He'd kept his peers in the dark for a reason. Opening that door would lead to more questions he didn't want to answer.

"I'm sorry that you have to come home to so many problems. Henry would not have wished this for you." Anna stared ahead of them, Chloe's tiny hand tucked in hers.

The kindness she'd shown him was undeserved. He should have accepted the punishment that was his alone long ago.

Noah shoved his misgivings aside for the moment. "Thank you for being there for my Mamm. She loves you and Chloe so much."

Her cheeks tinted pink. "I feel the same way about her. I lost Adam when I was quite young, and then my parents when I was still a teenager. At times, I hardly remember Adam." Regret filled her tone. "That makes me sad."

At the mention of her brother, all the old guilt returned. His foolish behavior all those years earlier had set in motion a chain of events that might never have taken place if he'd acted differently.

"Everything is going to be okay, Anna. I will make arrangements to hire some trustworthy men to work the farm. I won't leave you and my mother until I know you are taken care of."

The smile she gave him held a hint of sadness. He knew what she was thinking. "You must do what is best for you, Noah. If this life is no longer yours, then you must return to the one that is."

Her words mirrored his mother's earlier ones. He didn't answer. What was there to say?

Noah focused on the road ahead and let his thoughts run as free as the countryside around them. He knew every square inch of the land his family had owned for generations. He remembered plowing the fields with his Daed and his *Bruder*. Henry had kept his family fed through lean times and plentiful ones. He knew exactly what his Daed would say to him now. *Time to make a choice, Noah. Your family needs you. Time to come home.*

He brought the buggy to a stop in front of Anna's home. He climbed down and helped Chloe to the ground. She took off for the house.

"I'll take your bag inside for you," he murmured.

Going around to Anna's side, he held out his hand. She placed her hand in his and let him help her down. The second she was on the ground, she pulled her hand free. He sensed that he made her uneasy, and he wondered why.

"Come inside," she said in an unsteady voice. "I will make some tea to warm us up."

Anna didn't wait for his answer. She pivoted away and headed toward the house after her daughter. After a moment, he followed. His heart was beating a crazy rhythm against his chest, but he tamped it down. Being back in Rexford was bringing back so many emotions, but his training helped him control them. At least for now.

As he took her bag from the buggy and followed her up the steps to her house, he noticed one of the porch steps was loose. The railing was rotted away in several spots. How hard had Anna's life been since Joseph's passing?

She caught him surveying the area and held her head high. Anna would never ask for anyone's help—including his. Still, while he was here, he planned to offer.

Inside, Noah dropped the bag next to the door. A quick look around confirmed that plenty of things needed fixing in here as well. He promised himself he'd stay long enough to help Anna with the repairs. He owed that and so much more to his brother.

"Mason Burkholder comes around to help out when he can, but he has his own family to take care of, and finding the time is hard for him," Anna said in way of explanation. "You remember Mason from school?"

Noah did. Mason was a quiet young man who kept to himself. His mother had written a few years back that Mason had married. He hadn't missed her subtle reproach that he remained unattached.

Anna put the kettle on the propane-fueled cookstove. While she made tea, he made a fire to take the chill from the air.

He hadn't drunk tea since he'd left Rexford, but he accepted the cup she handed him.

"I'll check out your buggy today and see about fixing it."

She faced him across her tiny kitchen. "Thank you. I appreciate it. Though I won't be doing much driving until my wrist heals. And I don't know if I've ever thanked you properly for saving my life after the accident."

He shook his head. "You don't owe me any thanks. I'm glad I was there."

"Gött was watching out for me," she whispered. "He sent me you."

He was humbled that she believed he was sent from Gött, even though he didn't. Still, he hadn't been able to rid himself of the image of Anna lying in the snow on that deserted stretch of road. If he hadn't come along when he did, the outcome would have been far different. What if the person who'd run her off the road really had meant to harm her? And what if he'd returned before Noah got there?

Noah stepped closer. He could see she was struggling not to move away, and a bitter smile touched his mouth. "You're family, Anna. I'll always be there for you. I wish I had arrived sooner, before the accident."

Her gaze lingered on his face, and an old memory surfaced of a different time after Joseph's burial. He remembered thinking how vulnerable she appeared, mourning her husband's death, tears streaming down her cheeks. If all these incidents weren't accidents, then someone needed to pay for what they'd done to his family.

The vehicle likely belonged to a traveler passing through, but still, he planned to do a little checking around the area. If he could find the person responsible for the accident, maybe he could fit the pieces together as to why they had run Anna off the road. There had to be more to the story than a simple accident. Noah hadn't been able to get Dr. Montgomery's words out of his head, because they echoed his own thoughts. *One is an accident. Two is strange. Three . . . is something far worse.* Three was a pattern he didn't like.

"Have you remembered anything further about the vehicle that hit you?" he inquired again. He'd asked that morning, but maybe she'd recalled something in the hours that her brain had been awake.

Anna never broke eye contact as she shook her head. "The vehicle was bigger than a car, dark in color, and going very fast. I'm sorry. I wish I could remember more, but everything happened so suddenly. I was afraid I would die out there."

She was probably describing an SUV or a pickup truck. That narrowed it down a little at least.

He couldn't imagine the terror she'd gone through, and was still going through. It might be best to change the subject.

"Did you talk to my father much before his accident? Was he worried about anything?" *Great job, Noah. Way to pick something else awful for her.*

Anna stared at him, clearly taken aback. "No, not that I can remember. Henry wanted to get the loft repaired before springtime. He was worried he would be too busy with the planting to make the repairs at that time. And then the rains would come. I think the weight of trying to keep both houses running had him concerned as well."

Regret weighed on him once more. He'd let his father down in so many ways. "He didn't mention anything specific?"

She shook her head. "No, never. You know Henry. He kept his worries to himself."

That was his Daed. Never wanting to burden anyone. "Had you noticed anything out of the ordinary taking place around the house or in town recently?" He couldn't help but press the issue. He knew she didn't understand his line of questioning, but his training wouldn't allow him to let it go.

"I'm not sure I know what you mean." She frowned. "What's this about? Do you think Henry's death might not have been an accident after all?" The woman was perceptive.

Was he tilting at windmills? Searching for more to explain his Daed's passing besides a simple accident because he wasn't ready to accept it?

"I don't know. Perhaps I'm being paranoid, but I find it hard to believe my father would die in such a way. He was always so careful. He would never take unnecessary risks, like leaving work half-done the way it was in the loft."

Anna set her cup down. "I understand you don't want to believe his death happened that way. Sometimes the simplest answer is the hardest to accept," she said quietly.

His heart sank. She was right. But *nothing* about his father's death was easy to accept.

6

A few days later, Anna crossed to the window for the second time in less than an hour. March in many other parts of the country meant the beginning of springtime, but here in the western Rockies, winter left late, and it didn't show any sign of easing yet.

She'd spent the morning trying to finish the final quilt to take to Mrs. Schwartz's store so that she could begin working on the wall hanging for the upcoming Rexford Amish Community Auction that was scheduled in June. The proceeds would be used to help fund the local Amish school.

Yet, despite her good efforts, she'd admitted defeat. Without the use of her right hand, everything came out wrong, and she ended up having to pull out all the imperfect stitches, which unfortunately was most of them.

Anna put down her work and tried not to fret over money too much. Worry went against her faith. She needed to trust Gött and put aside her concerns.

Easier said than done.

Chloe had gone to spend the day with Mercy, and the house was quiet, giving Anna too much time to think. During moments like this, she felt Joseph's absence the most. Even when she was busy working on her quilts or at the Lathams' home, the days dragged by.

But the nights were the loneliest and the hardest to get through. She would wake up and reach for Joseph only to remember he was gone. She missed talking to him about the simple things in life. A hundred times a day, she'd think of something she wanted to share with him, like how big Chloe was getting, or something amusing she'd heard, and then she'd remember.

She'd been able to tell Joseph all her fears about the future, and he would simply smile and say Gött had a plan, and she should trust Him. If only she could find that much faith now when she needed it most. Facing the days without him was more than she could bear at times.

She jumped at an unexpected knock on her door. She was expecting Noah today, but she hadn't heard the buggy.

Anna peeked out the window. Mason Burkholder stood on her front porch. He hadn't been by in a few days.

She pulled the door open, happy for the interruption. "*Guder nammidaag*, Mason." He had been such a big help after Joseph's passing, and she enjoyed catching up with him about his family.

Mason held his hat in his hand. "Hello to you, Anna. I dropped by to see how you are feeling since the accident."

"Please come in and sit down. I'm fine. Danki for asking."

Mason sat on the bench she indicated. He seemed preoccupied. "You and your family have had such a hard time lately. Now, with Henry gone, how will you manage to keep the farm going?"

She was surprised by his words. "We'll be fine. Joseph's brother is back in town to help."

Mason's eyebrows rose. "He is? How long will he be staying?"

She wasn't sure how to answer the question. More importantly, why did Mason want to know so much? "I'm not sure."

"You know, if you and your family wanted to sell this place, I could help you out. I know some people."

This was the last thing she'd expected him to say. "Why would we want to sell? This is our home."

He jumped to his feet. "I was only thinking of you. No need to get upset. I should be going. Beth is waiting for me."

Before she could say a word, Mason rushed back out the door. She went to the window. He strode through the snow toward the woods that separated their property from the Millers' old place. The opposite direction from his home. Where was he going?

She watched until he disappeared into the woods, feeling unsettled. Mason had certainly acted strangely, but was she reading more into it than she should? He had always treated her and Joseph with kindness, even when Joseph was going through his shunning. Perhaps something was troubling him at home. That would certainly explain his unusual behavior. It was none of her business, but she would pray for him.

Anna dropped the curtain back in place and left her perch by the window. She added more wood to the fire to ease the chill that seemed to go straight through to her bones.

Outside, the noise of a buggy horse clopping along the icy path brought her mind off Mason's words. She retrieved her cloak and stepped out into the dreary afternoon. Noah was easing Mercy's mare Esther through the icy sludge.

He stopped by each day around this time since he'd fixed the damaged buggy for her and brought Marta home to her own barn. She was grateful for his help. He'd been repairing all the little things that Joseph used to take care of. Noah had a good heart, even though she suspected at times that he didn't see it.

When his buggy rounded the corner, he smiled and waved. She waved back, then smoothed her rumpled dress. She was being silly, but she found herself enjoying Noah's visits each day. Anna hadn't realized how deep her loneliness ran. With the exception of her friend Jessie's weekly visits and time spent with Mercy, she had been isolated in her grief.

"Whoa, Esther." Noah brought the mare to a halt out front and hopped down from his seat. She noticed he was still dressed in jeans and boots. No doubt he had a sweatshirt under his heavy winter coat. His head was uncovered. Since he'd purchased the clothing from Mrs. Schwartz's store, he had yet to wear any of the Amish garments. He wasn't home to stay, then. She wondered if he'd returned the clothes.

"How are you this afternoon?" He grinned at her from where he stood close to the buggy.

In many ways he reminded her of Joseph. Although they weren't similar in appearance, sometimes Noah would make a certain gesture, or say something that sounded exactly like Joseph. Yet their differences were as vast as the mountains behind her home. Joseph was a gentle soul. He could never have done the type of work that Noah did.

He must have caught something in her expression because his grin disappeared, and he asked, "What's wrong? Did something happen?"

She never was good at hiding her feelings. Joseph had always been able to guess when something was bothering her too.

Anna explained about the strange visit she'd had from Mason.

"What do you think he meant by that?" Noah's face was unreadable, no doubt a necessary skill in his line of work.

"I don't know. I've never seen him act like that before." She drew in a breath, letting go of the misgivings. Mason wasn't her concern. "You didn't have to brave the weather today, Noah. You can take a break from time to time, and I'm sure Mercy has things for you to do."

Did she sound ungrateful? She didn't want him to think she didn't appreciate all that he did for her. But she enjoyed his company a little too much, and she worried what would happen when he left again.

"I wanted to come. Mamm is busy playing games with Chloe. I had to get out of there before they roped me into playing hide-and-seek."

Anna laughed at the image that conjured up in her mind.

"Besides, I thought I'd finish repairing the kitchen cabinets today, since it looks like more snow is on the way. The outside work will have to wait."

"That would be nice," she said genuinely. "I'm not much good with a hammer."

His smile returned. "Well then, I'm glad I haven't forgotten how to swing one. Let me put Esther and the buggy in the barn, and I will be right back. You should go inside. It's cold."

She liked the way he said things. At times, Noah reverted to his native tongue, yet at others, his turn of a phrase was foreign to her. He was an unfolding mystery, one she'd never completely uncover, she suspected.

"I was getting ready to make some tea. Would you like some?"

He pretended to cringe, but she suspected he was playing. "To tell you the truth, I'm not much on tea anymore, but I would love some coffee."

Neither she nor Joseph had drunk *Kaffe*. "I'm sorry, but I don't have any."

He grinned at her as if he'd expected her answer. "That's okay. I bought some in town the other day. I know you don't usually have coffee, but I thought maybe you could give it a try this once."

No one in her family drank coffee growing up, and Joseph's family had preferred tea as well. Anna was pretty sure Noah had taken up the habit in the outside world.

She was willing to try, but not before throwing him a challenge of her own.

"I will give your coffee a try, if you agree to sample my apple fry pie." She remembered that once as a child, he'd found his mother's fresh-baked fry pies cooling in the kitchen, and he'd eaten so many he'd gotten sick. Since that time, Noah hadn't been able to touch another one.

The twinkle in his eyes swept her breath away. "You don't think I can do it, do you? Well, you're on. I'll be right back." He waved and led Esther to the barn.

Anna went back inside, took the pies out, and placed them on the baking sheet. She'd made them fresh that morning. Apple fry pies were Chloe's favorite as well.

Noah came inside as she placed the pies into the oven to heat. He closed the door and dropped his bag full of tools.

"Thank you for helping me out around here, Noah. I'm very grateful." And she was. In a short amount of time, he'd made some major improvements around the place. She couldn't imagine doing all the things he had.

He dismissed her gratitude with a shrug. "It's nothing. I enjoy working with my hands."

Anna had seen all the hard work he'd done on the kitchen cabinets, yet like his Daed, he was a humble man.

"Do you want me to boil some water?" She had never prepared the drink before, so she had no idea where begin.

He pretended to be appalled by her question. "I have just the thing to make the task much easier." Noah brought something from his bag. She recognized it. A percolator. "Now, watch carefully, so you'll know how to make it in the future," he teased. The future. She didn't let herself read too much into that statement. He'd made it clear he'd be leaving again, though he hadn't said when.

He poured water into the pot and added some of the ground coffee into the filter before reassembling the pot and placing it on the stovetop.

"Now what?" she asked

"Now we wait."

Anna forgot all about the coffee as her heart drummed a crazy beat.

Had she become such a recluse that she didn't know how to act when someone visited her home? *Calm down. It's just Noah.*

He went to retrieve his tools. "This will take a few minutes. I'll get started on the cabinet while we wait."

Anna pretended to be busy herself by putting away her quilting supplies. Her hands shook so much that she ended up just shoving the supplies into her bag rather than putting them away neatly.

Before long, the kitchen was filled with the scent of fresh coffee—which Anna actually found that she enjoyed—and apple fry pies warming in the oven.

Once Noah finished the cabinet he'd been working on, he laid the tools down. "Your fry pies smell wonderful. I'll go wash up."

While he was gone, Anna placed the pies on a dish, and then got out two cups and stared at them. She wasn't sure how Noah liked his coffee.

"Here, let me help you." She didn't realize he was there until he spoke. He came to where she stood next to the percolator and poured the hot brew into the cups. "Now, I prefer mine black, but some people like milk and sugar. Maybe you should try those for your first time?"

How odd she must seem, a grown woman who had never tried a cup of coffee before. She found herself chuckling.

"What's so funny?" Noah asked.

"Us. We're so funny. What do you suppose people would say if they saw me trying coffee for the first time at my age?"

He joined in the laughter. "They would probably wonder what took you so long. Many people in the English world can hardly function without it."

She handed him the plate of pies and brought some sugar and milk to the table.

After pouring a generous amount of each into her cup, Anna tentatively sipped the liquid. She closed her eyes. It was quite good.

"You like it?" Noah watched her expression.

Anna nodded. "I do." She pointed to the pies. "Your turn."

She so hoped he liked her fry pie. *Wouldn't it be terrible if they made him sick again?*

One bite and his face relaxed into a smile. "They are delicious, but I have a confession to make. I never ate too many of Mamm's fry pies. I actually threw them all away."

He waited for her to respond. It was a moment before she could form the question. "You threw them away? Why?"

"Because fry pies are the one thing my Mamm can't make. Daed felt the same way, as did Joseph, but we never had the heart to tell her. Yours, on the other hand, are wonderful." He took another bite, then wiped a crumb away. "But if you tell her I said as much, I will deny it to the bitter end."

She couldn't help but beam at the compliment. "That's high praise. I'm glad you like them. And don't worry—your secret is safe with me."

Something she couldn't begin to explain crossed his face. He finished the pie and took another. She enjoyed having him here to talk to. With just her and Chloe, most of their conversations were simple ones. Anna sipped her coffee and realized she hadn't thought about the things that needed to be done, or her money problems, since he'd arrived.

Noah gazed out the window. "The snow is starting to come down harder. I'd better finish up, and then I'll fetch Chloe and bring her safely home."

Anna, he knew, didn't understand why Noah was so reluctant to return to Rexford. This community was the only place she would ever call home.

But for him, most everything he loved about the community as a child was gone. His brother. His friend Adam. Now his Daed.

Yet if he were truly honest with himself, the thrill of his job with the CIA was fading with each moment he spent living the plain life. Almost as if his former life had been here all these years, waiting for him to return.

Although he'd barely been here a week, already he'd settled easily into the simple routine of the Amish way of life. He enjoyed the time he had with his Mamm, and his and Anna's quiet talks while he repaired little things around the house were something he looked forward to each day. Not to mention the time he got to spend with his niece.

Noah cast a worried glance outside as the snow continued to fall harder. He hated thinking of Anna and Chloe here alone in such weather.

As he gathered his tools, he had an idea. "Why don't you come stay with Mamm tonight? I know she would love having you both there. I can bring you home tomorrow once the weather clears."

Anna seemed ready to reject his suggestion. "I don't know. Chloe and I would be putting you out of your room again, and you've only settled in."

He liked the way she put others ahead of herself, but he wanted to take care of her for a change. "I don't mind. I can bed down in the great room by the fire just as easily. Besides, a big storm is coming this way tonight. I don't like thinking about you and Chloe here by yourselves."

"Are you sure?"

"I am."

"Oke. I'll go pack some things for myself and Chloe." She hurried away. Noah carried his tools to the door. The tiny house she and Joseph had shared was in much better shape with the new repairs. He was proud of the work he'd done. He believed his father would be as well.

While he waited for her to pack, Noah couldn't help but wonder what would happen to Anna once he left the community again. Would she remarry? The thought of her with someone else was not a pleasing one.

He forced the thought aside. When she returned, he took her bag and his tools. "Why don't you wait here where it's warm? I'll go get Esther and the buggy and bring them around. While I'm in the barn, I'll make sure Marta and the cows have plenty of food and water to last." He hurried out into the chilly evening and tossed her bag up onto the seat along with his tools before feeding the animals. Then he harnessed Esther as quickly as he could and walked her around to the front of the house.

Once Anna was seated next to him, he urged the mare toward his home.

Noah hadn't been able to get his gut reaction to his Daed's death out of his head. His Mamm and Anna saw things differently than he did, due to his training. They looked for the good in people. But sometimes bad people hid their evil deeds under the pretense of good.

He'd driven his car to the site of Anna's accident the day after it occurred. After a close examination of the scene, he'd found no evidence that the driver had tried to apply the brakes at all. If Noah could find the vehicle that hit her, there would be damage to the front bumper, he was pretty sure. That would be enough proof to go to the sheriff's office.

While he was almost positive that Anna's accident was in some way related to his Daed's death, he couldn't help wondering if the trouble had started much earlier, with Joseph's passing.

Noah had debated for days on the best way to broach the subject with Anna. Now, he decided just to ask. "I know this is probably something you don't want to talk about, but do you mind if I ask you some questions about Joseph's . . . accident?"

Anna turned in her seat, a furrow forming between her eyebrows. After a second, she nodded. "This is not an easy topic for me to discuss still, but I will try to answer your questions. What do you want to know?"

"I was wondering if you remembered anything strange happening in the days before Joseph's death. Something he might have mentioned to you." He should let the whole thing go and accept what everyone was telling him, but he couldn't. Something didn't add up in his mind.

"What do you mean? You think Joseph's death was something more than an accident too?"

He didn't have any proof to substantiate his feeling. "I'm not saying that at all. I was wondering what Joseph was doing at the Millers' farm." That was something that he'd never understood. At the time, he'd been too grief-stricken to ask.

"Oh," she said, and her troubled expression cleared. "He was looking at the property to buy it. He and your father had put a down payment on it. They had an agreement with Mrs. Miller before she passed away. Joseph was going to plant the following spring."

He wasn't sure he'd heard her correctly. His Daed had never mentioned wanting to buy the Miller place before. "I had no idea. What happened to the agreement after Joseph passed away?"

She shrugged. "I guess their arrangement ended. After Joseph died, Henry couldn't keep up with the payments."

Why hadn't his Mamm mentioned the purchase before? "Does the property still belong to the Miller family?"

"I don't know. To be honest, I haven't thought about the place since that time."

Noah nodded, his thoughts churning. He would speak to his Mamm the following day to see if she knew anything more, then go to the Miller farm and check things out for himself.

Esther rounded the curve in the road, and the house appeared before them. With the weather conditions getting worse by the minute, he breathed a sigh of relief at the sight.

In the past, he remembered how coming home had always brought a smile to his face. No matter how tired he was, seeing the family home had a way of making him feel better.

He'd once loved this community. The land. His home. But that was before Adam's death. And that felt like a lifetime ago.

Noah stopped the buggy and hopped off. Once Anna was on the ground, he said, "Go inside and get out of the cold. I'll bring your bag in once the horse is taken care of."

He started to leave, but she reached out and clasped his arm, keeping him there. He could read every single one of her fears in her eyes, and he gently touched her cheek.

"Don't worry. If I find out anything, I'll let you know. Right now, it's just a hunch that won't go away. Go get warm."

She watched him with those haunted eyes for the longest time before she turned and walked away.

Noah blew out the breath he'd held inside. Lately he'd been noticing little things about Anna that he hadn't in the past. How her smile lit up her face and made her eyes dance. How soft her skin was where he'd touched her face.

Frustrated with himself, he climbed back into the buggy and urged Esther toward the barn. Once he had unhitched the mare, he led her inside and brushed her down. He had almost forgotten how much he loved working with the animals. He'd finished the repairs to the floor above the day before. Working on the same area where his

Daed had died was difficult, but he owed it to Henry to keep things going while he was here.

As he brushed, Noah found himself struggling against the urgings of his heart. He was needed here. His Mamm had pleaded with him to stay this time. Chloe could use a male figure in her life now as well, and Anna needed his help. Yet every time he looked at Anna, he remembered her pain at losing her brother, for which he alone was responsible.

"Gött, I need help. I don't know what to do," he whispered into the silence of the barn. His only answer was the occasional neighing of Esther.

He was being foolish. He wasn't deserving of Gött's attention, much less His mercy and guidance.

Once Esther was secured in her stall, he trudged through the falling snow to the front door, shaking the snow from his feet before he opened it.

Noah stepped inside and froze at the sight before him. Anna and Chloe were seated next to the fire, Anna reading to her daughter. His mother was close by, her eyes closed, listening to the story. The cozy family scene made clear all the things missing from his life.

He had written off having a family of his own because of the type of work he did. Anonymity was crucial, putting down roots impossible. But right from the beginning of his work at the CIA, he knew that the type of work the agency did went against the things he'd once believed in. Noah was at constant war with himself.

"Onkel Noah!" Chloe exclaimed when she spotted him at the door. She jumped from her Mamm's lap and ran into his open arms. He couldn't imagine loving this child more if she were his own. She was the spitting image of Anna, and she stole a little more of his heart with each passing day.

"Did you finally wear out your Grossmammi, Chloe?"

The little girl giggled at the way he talked. Noah knew he was like someone who lived in another country to her, as he alternated between the Amish dialect and the English.

"You sound funny," she told him.

"I do?" He ruffled her hair and set her down. She quickly climbed back on her Mamm's lap.

"I am quite capable of keeping up with my *Kinskind*, Noah." Though Mercy tried to sound stern, the smile on her face gave her away.

"There's dinner waiting for you. Anna ate already." Mercy rose and led him to the kitchen.

Even before she set the bowl in front of him, he knew his Mamm had made one of his favorites. He'd watched her prepare the thick beef-and-noodle oven stew for family and company through the years. The simple Amish meals his mother prepared were a welcome relief from the food he usually grabbed on the run. So many times, he'd end up eating something unhealthy simply because it was fast and he was hungry.

He dug into the bowl with relish. "This is delicious," he said in between mouthfuls.

Mercy sat beside him, clearly pleased by his appetite. "Beef and noodles always was one of your favorites. I am glad to see that hasn't changed."

Noah stopped chewing. He could tell that the loss of her husband and son had taken their toll on her. There was a weariness embedded in her face that nothing could ever remove. Guilt tugged at his heart once more. What would happen to her and Anna if he left again? No doubt the community would come to their aid, but it wasn't the same as having one's family there. He was her family. She needed *him*.

But how could he face that guilt every day? Or worse, risk losing her by confessing why he'd really left?

7

Outside, the noise of a vehicle coming to a stop in front of her home made Anna frown. Since he'd been home she hadn't seen Noah use his car, yet someone was outside, and the hour was still very early.

Anna peeked out through the curtains. Edward was walking up the steps to her house. What on earth was he doing here?

"Stay here, Chloe. I'll only be a minute."

She slipped out the door and closed it behind her. In all the time she'd worked for Edward, he had never visited her at home.

"Anna—" Edward stopped on the step and stared at her wrist. "Oh, my dear child, I had no idea you were hurt so badly."

She tried to reassure him. "No, please, don't worry. The injury isn't so bad, and the swelling is going down every day. I am fine, really. Please come in."

He stayed rooted where he was. "Oh my goodness. I blame myself. I should have insisted on driving you home." The man seemed distraught.

Anna did not know what to say other than to reassure him once again that she was going to be fine.

The familiar sound of a buggy sloshing down the snowy road to her house made Anna glance up. Noah coming her way was a welcome sight. She wasn't sure why Edward was so upset, but she was feeling decidedly uncomfortable.

Edward lifted his head. When he spotted the buggy approaching, he started. "I'm sorry. I didn't realize you had company coming. I should go."

Before she could stop him, he went down the steps to an SUV parked sideways in her yard and drove away.

Noah jumped down and came up the steps, a concerned look on his face. "What was that about?" he asked.

Anna shook her head. "I'm not really sure. That was Edward. When he saw my injured wrist, he blamed himself for what happened." She shook her head. "I told him I would be okay."

"Does he normally show up at your house?"

Anna shook her head. "No, not at all. His visit was . . . odd."

"What's odd?" Chloe appeared behind her.

Anna beamed down at her daughter. "Nothing. Are you and your Onkel ready to start work?" Anna changed the subject, not wanting Chloe to see that she was worried. Something had been different about Edward's behavior.

"We are," Noah said. "And we'd better get started. I'll just put the buggy away first." He peered down at Chloe with a serious expression. "I thought we could repair the doorframe in the sitting room next."

Anna smiled as Chloe nodded solemnly. She remembered how much Chloe had loved helping Joseph work.

Once Noah and Chloe were busy, Anna worked the dough to make the homemade pizza that was to be a surprise for Chloe, even though the task was difficult with one hand. While she clumsily rolled out the dough with her good hand in the middle of the rolling pin, she couldn't get Edward's strange behavior out of her head. She felt terrible that the sweet old man was so worried about her, but he had nothing to feel guilty about.

With the crust ready on the pan, Anna prepared her homemade rustic tomato sauce, then topped it with fresh mozzarella and Parmesan cheese, bits of sausage and pepperoni, along with onions, mushrooms, and peppers. Chopping the ingredients had not been easy, but she could do it, unlike the precision work of her quilts. She covered the pizza with more cheese from Mrs. Schwartz, popped the pan into the oven, then set the table and poured three glasses of cold milk from Sunshine.

"Something smells delicious, and I am hungry." Noah poked his head around the corner fifteen minutes later and watched her take the pizza from the oven.

She smiled over her shoulder. "Homemade pizza, and I'm glad you're hungry, because it's ready."

He returned her smile. "I'll get Chloe."

Anna cut three slices of the pizza and put them on plates and carried them to the table.

"Pizza!" Chloe exclaimed and ran to the table.

"Prayers first," Anna reminded her daughter as the three of them sat down.

"Guess what, Mamm?" Chloe said the second the prayer ended. "We finished the doorframe already."

"You did? That's great. You two make a great team." She leaned over and kissed her daughter's cheek and smiled at Noah. He was incredibly patient with Chloe, who wanted to help her Onkel with all his tasks. Chloe loved being with him, and he seemed to enjoy the time he had with his niece.

In the short time he had been helping around the place, many things had been accomplished. The house was almost back to normal. She realized she'd miss their time together when he finished.

Once the meal was cleared away, Anna watched as Noah gathered his tools and got ready to leave. He handed Chloe the hammer, which she proudly carried to the door.

Noah kneeled in front of Chloe. "Thank you for helping me today, Kind. I couldn't have finished repairing the doorframe so quickly without you."

Beaming from the compliment, Chloe hugged his neck. "Are you coming to church with us tomorrow, Onkel Noah?" The question surprised them both and Noah's gaze flew to Anna.

"Chloe, that's not nice," Anna gently chided her daughter. Chloe didn't understand that Noah might be hesitant to go to church with them. She loved attending the service, and it was a staple in her life.

"Do you really want me to attend?" Noah asked Chloe.

Chloe nodded. "Ja. I will miss you if you don't."

Noah's swallow was visible. Chloe's words seemed to melt his heart as they had Anna's. "Then I will try to come. For you."

The child hugged him tight.

Over the top of Chloe's head, his gaze held Anna's. She didn't know what to say. She was humbled that he was willing to attend the service for Chloe. The question was whether it would be allowed.

Noah let the little girl go and rose to his feet, retrieving his coat off a peg on the wall. "I'll see you both tomorrow." He headed outside and closed the door without another word.

"Chloe, I'll be right back. Stay in here where it's warm." Anna followed Noah out into the wintry afternoon.

Noah still stood on the front porch, staring at the distant mountains.

Anna closed the door and approached him. He turned and gazed at her. The battle she saw inside him broke her heart.

"You don't have to come with us tomorrow, Noah. I'll explain to Chloe. Don't feel obligated because she asked you to go. Chloe can be persistent at times, and she loves you very much." She'd been more than a little surprised when he'd agreed to go.

His pained expression told her he was struggling with the decision. "I know, and I want to come for Chloe's sake, but to be honest with you, I haven't attended church in years. Since I left Rexford. I'm not sure I will be welcomed anymore."

She was quick to disagree. "That's not true. You may have been gone for a while, but everyone knows you, and I promise you will be welcomed if you choose to come tomorrow. After all, you were not excommunicated." She could see that he didn't fully believe her. Anna had sensed something deeper troubling him on several occasions. She'd seen the distant look in his eyes, but she was too afraid that it was something related to his terrifying job to ask him about it.

He attempted a smile. "I should get going. I have an errand to run before I head home." Up above, the skies threatened more snow. "Hopefully, the weather will hold off for a while longer."

In the distance, the jingling of a bridle could be heard, drawing Noah's attention to the path. "Are you expecting company?" he asked, no doubt remembering Edward's visit earlier.

Anna spotted Jessie's buggy heading their way and nodded. "Yes, my friend Jessie is stopping by to help me finish my final quilt to take to Mrs. Schwartz. I can't get much work done with this." She held up her injured hand. Just making lunch with one hand had taken twice as long as normal. "You remember Jessie, don't you?"

"I do. The two of you were always playing with those faceless dolls of yours." He smiled down at her.

"Yes, we were. Now Jessie has a house full of *Kinner*, and I have my Chloe. And they all still play with the same dolls we used to play with. Chloe loves them." Anna couldn't keep the catch out of her voice. She and Joseph had planned on having a house full of Kinner themselves. If they'd had more time together, would Gött have blessed them with more children?

She caught Noah watching her with sympathy written on his face. "I miss him too," he said quietly, and she thought she saw tears in his eyes.

Jessie brought her horse to a halt in front of the house. The black-topped buggy had barely come to a stop before five little girls of various ages scrambled down and ran up the steps to where Noah and Anna stood.

They all stopped to gape at the stranger.

"Girls, this is Noah Petersheim, Chloe's Onkel. Noah, this is Mary, Emma, Susan, Martha, and Mae." Anna indicated each girl.

"Nice to meet you, ladies," he said.

All five girls, each a smaller version of her mother, parroted, "Nice to meet you too."

Jessie cleared the last step and shooed her girls into the house. "That's enough gawking. Go inside and play with Chloe."

The girls did as their mother asked and left the adults alone.

Anna hadn't spoken to Jessie about Noah being back in town, but word had clearly spread around the community, as her friend didn't seem a bit surprised to see him.

"Noah, how are you? I was sorry to hear about Henry. He will be missed in the community." Jessie held her hand out to him and they shook hands.

"Danki, Jessie. Nice to see you again." He faced Anna. "I will see you tomorrow." He didn't wait for her response, but strode down the steps and toward the barn. He was such a troubled soul that her heart went out to him.

She became aware that Jessie was watching her stare after Noah, and Anna placed her hands on her cheeks to hide the color growing there.

"Come inside out of the cold." Anna ignored Jessie's arched brows and reached for the door. After another curious glance at the barn, Jessie followed her inside.

Jessie took her time unfastening her cloak and traveling bonnet before placing them on pegs by the door. Anna heard Noah leave. She went to the window and waved as he drove past the house. He was heading in the opposite direction from his home. He'd said he had an errand to run. Where might he be going this afternoon?

When she turned around, Jessie was standing behind her. Anna could read every one of her worries before she voiced them aloud.

"He's not one of us anymore, Anna. He won't be the person you need him to be."

Forcing herself to look her friend in the eye took everything inside Anna. "I don't know what you're talking about. Noah is my family. That's all." She lifted her chin and dared Jessie to say more.

Jessie held up her hands. "I hope you know what's best for you. Now, where is this lovely quilt that needs finishing?"

Anna pointed, and her friend made a beeline for the quilt Anna had left on the sofa. Her fingers trailed over the fabric.

"The songbird quilt you finished earlier was my favorite, but this double wedding ring-and-star design is lovely. Using deep red and greens for the star and rings was a good choice. And you were so close to being finished."

Anna brought over her quilting supplies. "Ja. I had planned to have the quilt finished on the day after the accident, but . . ."

Jessie brought out the needed supplies and got to work on the final pieces of the quilt. "Such a dreadful thing to happen. How have you been feeling?"

"I'll be back to normal soon enough." Anna sat next to her friend and watched Jessie making neat stitches effortlessly.

"I know the Lathams miss you." She shook her head. "Henderson's Curve is very dangerous. There have been so many accidents there over the years."

Anna hesitated. Did she dare voice Noah's suspicions—her own suspicions?

Jessie glanced up from her quilting. "What is it?"

Anna spoke quietly. "Noah doesn't think what happened was an accident."

Jessie eyed her, then appeared to choose her words carefully. "He sees things differently because of his job. Why would someone want to hurt you? There are only good people here and around Rexford."

Was Jessie right? Was Noah seeing what had happened to her and Henry through jaded eyes?

Noah found himself thinking about Anna's smile. Even when they weren't together, he could see it. He loved the way her face shone and her green eyes danced. She was a compassionate woman, and she'd come to occupy way too much of his time lately. He was here in Rexford for a purpose—to help his mother hire some men to get through the spring planting—and then he would return to his own life.

So why was the thought of leaving Anna and his family again so hard to consider?

Noah turned Esther toward the Miller farm down the road from Anna's house.

When Anna had told him Joseph and his father planned to buy the Miller place, he'd been dumbfounded. Of course it made sense to expand their farm with abutting land. But why keep it secret?

He spotted the entrance to the Millers' place and pulled Esther to a halt. He'd expected to see an overgrown, abandoned piece of property, but that wasn't the case. Someone had definitely done some work here. Land had been cleared away to allow heavy equipment in. Several portable buildings were set up. What exactly was the new owner planning to do with the farm?

Today, the place was empty of activity, the gate closed and locked. Noah urged Esther down the road, closer to the gate. Heavy equipment was everywhere.

Without actually trespassing past the gate—though he considered it—there was nothing more for him to see. He headed the buggy for home. He'd call Robert Tenley, a fellow CIA agent, and have him do some checking into who had bought the Miller property, maybe find out when they'd moved into the area and what they were planning. Because what he'd seen here today had him more concerned than ever. He couldn't help thinking that whatever was going on here had something to do with his brother's and father's deaths.

8

Why was the house so cold? Anna roused herself the next morning, though it was difficult to leave the warmth and comfort of her bed. *The stove must have gone out.* But she'd stoked it the night before, and the heat should have lasted longer than this. She dressed quickly and went downstairs.

A breeze came from near the front door. The window near the door was shattered, pieces of glass scattered around the floor. How had that happened? Had some animal tried to gain entrance during the night? Just last week, Noah had told her he'd spotted a black bear near their place. She suppressed a shiver. Would the bear keep coming back?

She swept up the glass before Chloe could step on some, then called to her daughter to wake up. "Chloe, get up and get dressed. Put a shawl around your shoulders and come downstairs for breakfast."

"Is Onkel Noah here yet?" Chloe called. Anna heard her little feet on the floorboards above.

"Not yet, but soon."

Chloe went to the kitchen and found a cardboard box and some tape to cover the broken window. She would have to ask Noah to help her with a permanent repair. While she worked, Jessie's gentle words of caution came to mind once more as they had many times since yesterday. Jessie meant well, but there was no need for the warning.

Sure, since he'd been home, she and Noah had spent a lot of time together. But he was only there to help her with the repairs around the house. Anna loved the time they shared together, and she was grateful that he spent time with Chloe as well. He was being a good uncle and brother-in-law. Nothing more. If only she could get him out of her head. He was in her thoughts constantly. She recalled each of their conversations and would find herself laughing at something he'd said for no particular reason.

She hadn't laughed much since Joseph passed away. Thinking about the hole that would appear in her life and Chloe's when Noah left scared her. The little girl had grown close to her Onkel.

Anna finished the makeshift repair to the window and put the tape back in the drawer.

Today, Noah would be attending the church service with them at the farm of the Stoltzfuses, the family chosen to host the service. Anna was a little anxious for him. The members of this community usually extended a welcoming hand to anyone who wanted to attend church. The Amish didn't believe in turning anyone away. But Noah wasn't just anyone. He was a former Amish man who had walked away from his community, his family, and his faith. Some in the congregation might not be so forgiving of that.

Please help him.

Chloe came downstairs. "What happened to the window? Is that why it's so cold?"

"Yes, that's why it's so cold. Maybe a bird flew into it. Here, eat your eggs." If Anna pretended she wasn't worried, hopefully Chloe wouldn't be worried. A bird was far less frightening than a bear.

It worked. Anna was spared telling another white lie as Chloe dug into her breakfast. Just as they were finishing, the *clip-clop* of a horse's hooves sounded from outside. She helped Chloe into her coat and together they went out in time to see Noah rein the mare to a stop in front of her house. Seated beside him and beaming with happiness was his Mamm. Anna couldn't remember the last time she'd seen Mercy so pleased. Noah attending church service with her obviously meant a lot.

He hopped down and helped Mercy to her feet. There was something different about him.

Anna realized with delight that he'd chosen to wear the clothes he'd purchased from Mrs. Schwartz. He was so handsome in the black broadfall pants, the simple blue shirt peeking out from the collar of his coat and bringing out the blue in his eyes.

Mercy greeted both Anna and Chloe with hugs. "A beautiful day for the service, don't you think? Spring is in the air." Mercy's joy showed on her face, and Anna was happy to see her mother-in-law smiling.

"Ja," Anna said, returning her smile. Perhaps the winter days of their lives were starting to fade as well.

Noah chucked Chloe under the chin. "And how are you this morning, Chloe?"

Chloe beamed up at him. "*Gut.* I'm glad you're coming with us to church."

Noah's gaze fell on Anna. He removed his hat with a solemn expression. "And how are you?"

While Jessie's earlier warning played through her head, Anna couldn't help smiling. She was happy that Noah was here. She would worry about the future when the time came.

Anna smiled up at him. "I am well. You look very nice."

He appeared slightly embarrassed. "Danki. I figured today would be a good day to wear them." There was a waver to his voice that wasn't usually there. Was he nervous about attending church today?

She wanted to make him feel at ease. "You made a wise choice. Today *is* a good day for them."

He noticed the patched window for the first time. "What happened there?" Alarm was clear in his voice.

"I'm not sure. I think perhaps an animal tried to get in during the night. I've patched the glass for now. It should hold for a while."

She could tell he had doubts, but he didn't voice them in front of Chloe. "I'll nail some wood over it after church. That should keep whatever it was out. When I go into town next, I'll get another pane of glass to replace that one."

She nodded gratefully. "I'll be right back. I need to get the food I prepared for the after-church meal." Anna headed to the kitchen table where she'd set the five-in-one casserole that consisted of hamburger, onion, spaghetti, peas, tomato juice, and cheese all cooked together to make the traditional Amish after-church meal. Though her wrist was almost back to normal, she'd still had to recruit Chloe for some of the simpler tasks for the dish.

Her fingers trailed along the smooth wood of the table Joseph had made for her as a wedding gift. She still remembered how proud he'd been when he presented it to her.

"Ready?" Noah watched her closely, no doubt seeing the turmoil inside her. She hadn't realized he'd followed her inside.

She faced him and nodded. "Yes, I'm ready."

Noah took the dish from her, and together they went outside.

Anna climbed up next to Mercy, and Noah handed her the casserole dish, then helped Chloe into the buggy. Once he was at the reins, they headed out of town to the Stoltzfus farm north of Rexford. The service today would take place in their great room. The Stoltzfus home was large enough for the congregation to fit inside comfortably.

As they pulled into the entrance leading to the farm, Anna could see the buggies lined up close to the barn. There was little time to spare before the service started.

She, Chloe, and Mercy went inside.

Mrs. Stoltzfus was a kind woman who welcomed everyone into her home. "Anna, you are improved since the accident?"

Anna set the casserole down on the kitchen table next to the rest of the food. "Much better. My wrist is almost healed. I should be fine to go back to work tomorrow."

"Thanks be to Gött you weren't hurt worse." Mrs. Stoltzfus tsked with concern.

Before Anna could comment, Jessie and her girls arrived, and Anna was grateful to have the attention off herself, but she still remembered the difference of opinion she and Jessie had the previous day.

Jessie clasped Anna's hand. "We should take our seats before the unmarried men come in. You'll all sit next to us?"

Anna nodded and squeezed her friend's hand, glad there were no ill feelings.

They found their seats as the men filed in, followed by the unbaptized youth and boys and then Noah. The men were seated on one side of the room and women on the other, facing each other as was the custom of their district.

Anna couldn't take her eyes off Noah. Even from where she sat, she could tell he felt ill at ease. She had no idea what struggles he was facing in his heart, but she said a silent prayer that Gött would show him a clear path to being free of them.

To start the service, one of the elder men led with a song from the *Ausbund* hymnal, carrying the first few notes before all others joined in.

When the second song ended, Mr. Stoltzfus, who was a deacon, read from the Bible, and then the bishop stood in front of the group to deliver the sermon.

"Gött asks for our obedience," Bishop Eicher said in the Amish dialect. "We may face things in life we do not understand, but if we put our trust in Gött and let Him direct our steps, then He will show us the path we are to follow. He will bless our lives."

As Anna listened to Bishop Eicher talk about being obedient to Gött in all circumstances of life, tears welled up. She had lost her way when Joseph died, struggling to get back on the path with so much to bear. No matter how lonely she felt, she wasn't alone and never had been. Gött was right there with her all the way.

Bishop Abraham Eicher had been serving the church for as long as Noah could remember. When he was younger, Noah had listened to the sermons but hadn't really applied them to his life. Now he felt as if the bishop were speaking directly to him.

Noah swallowed hard, but he couldn't rid himself of the despair that had formed in his throat. He hadn't felt as if he belonged anywhere since he'd left Rexford all those years ago. Was a second chance with Gött possible? With his family? With his former community? Surely it was too much to hope for.

The men had mostly been polite but a little guarded. He understood why. Many didn't remember him from when he lived here, and those who did probably recalled the shunning that Joseph had gone through. He'd caught a few suspicious looks during the service. Their distrust assured him he had a hard road ahead to gain their support, even without knowing the secrets he kept inside. When they did, would he be turned away? Unlike his brother, he couldn't be shunned—he hadn't been baptized. But people could make it uncomfortable for him.

With the service over, the meal would probably last for hours while people socialized. Noah found himself fielding many questions about his past and whether or not he'd come home to stay. The experience was a difficult one and he found himself wishing for Anna's gentle presence close by, but the men and women ate separately.

Once the meal was finally finished, the men worked together to clear away the benches. Noah lifted one end of a bench while Lemuel Troyer, Jessie's husband, took the other. He hadn't seen Lemuel since their school days together.

"Good to have you back, Noah," Lemuel told him once the cleanup was finished and every bench was stored away. "You should come to dinner at our home sometime soon."

Noah was humbled by the offer. He and Lemuel had once been friends. "I would like that."

"*Gut.* How about Saturday evening?"

Although Lemuel was a few years younger, he had been a good-natured youth growing up. Noah could see that same jovial personality in the grown-up version.

Noah smiled. "That sounds nice."

Lemuel spotted his wife and girls coming his way. "We will see you then," he said, and he and his family headed to their wagon.

Noah watched as Lemuel helped each of his girls into the family wagon, which was designed to allow parents and children to sit inside it. The wagon had windows in the back so the driver could see behind him clearly when he turned his head. Lemuel donned his hat and then waved as he and his family left the farm.

Noah didn't see his Mamm or Anna anywhere. He'd wait for them by the buggy. They were probably finishing up the clearing away inside the house.

As he leaned against the buggy, the warmth of the sun felt good on his face, a sharp contrast to the nip in the air. He'd dreaded the service, unsure of the reaction he'd get. The experience had been as painful as he'd expected, except for the unexpected kindness Lemuel had shown him. He couldn't help but remember the way he'd once fit into the community.

"Onkel Noah!" He opened his eyes to see Chloe bounding toward him. She was excited about their promised afternoon skating trip, and he found himself catching her enthusiasm.

He scooped her up into his arms. "Where are your Mamm and Grossmammi?"

"They're coming. Grossmammi had to say goodbye to Mrs. Stoltzfus, and they love to talk."

Noah chuckled at the child's directness. "And you're in a hurry to get to the pond."

Chloe nodded eagerly. "There they are. Let's go."

As much as he wanted to go for his niece, he could feel all the old fears resurfacing. He'd relived that day at the pond with Adam in his mind countless times. His own foolish goading had caused his friend's death. Shoving those painful memories aside took everything inside him, but he did it because he was determined to be strong for Chloe.

"Are you sure you won't come with us?" Noah asked his mother on the ride home. He hated thinking of her being alone at the house. *After you leave, she'll be alone most of the time.* The unbidden thought stung him.

Mercy shook her head. "Nay, I think I will go lie down for a bit. You three go and have fun. But first, let me make you some hot chocolate to ease the cold of the day."

Her response was expected, and he smiled a little sadly. "That sounds nice."

Mercy patted his arm. "Don't worry, Soh, spring is on the way. Soon the snow will melt and the planting will begin. Then you'll want lemonade instead of cocoa."

This was not the conversation he wanted to have. He'd had no luck with finding men to help with the planting. He wasn't sure what to do next.

Once Mercy made the hot chocolate and handed Noah the thermos, she kissed each of them goodbye. "I will see you all soon." She waved as they left.

"I wish she would have come with us," Anna said, her own misgivings evident in her tone. "I think she would have enjoyed the outing."

"Me too. She can be a stubborn woman at times." Noah tried to push aside his constant worry for his mother and enjoy the day. He adored Chloe, but the extra time he spent with Anna was even more enjoyable. More and more lately, he found himself daydreaming about her. When he was doing the chores around the farm, her face had a way of showing up. But no matter how attracted he was to her, they could never be. He wasn't plain anymore.

Noah hadn't been to Emerson's Pond since he was a kid. Yet as he stopped the buggy close by, nothing appeared to have changed. He swallowed back the dread he felt inside and hopped down. This wasn't the same place where Adam had died, and he wasn't the same person.

"Are you really going to skate with us?" Chloe asked her Mamm as if she couldn't believe it were true.

Anna laughed at her daughter's enthusiasm. "Yes, I'm really skating." She went to the bench near the edge of the pond to put on her skates.

"When was this bench put in?" Noah asked.

"A few years back. Levi Weaver wanted the Kinner to have a place to sit and take off their skates. Or put worms on their fishing poles."

"Very nice." Noah admired the craftsmanship before he stooped down and helped Chloe lace her skates. Then he put his on with fingers that trembled a little.

Anna was struggling to lace hers up as well.

"Here, let me help you." Noah knelt next to her and snugged the laces tight. "How does that feel?"

When she didn't answer, he peered up into her beautiful face and lost himself in her eyes.

She drew in a deep breath and gave a tiny nod, shaking him out of his trance.

He rose to his feet and held out his hand. "Don't worry. I promise I won't let you fall."

She clasped his hand, and he pulled her to her feet.

"Stay put," he told them. "I need to go see if the ice is safe. It's a good, clear blue, which is promising, but I still want to measure the thickness."

Anna understood the extra precautions and appreciated them.

Noah produced a small auger and measuring tape. He drilled through the ice in one area and lowered the measuring tape into the hole, hooking it on the bottom of the ice. He breathed a sigh of relief. "Five inches. That's plenty safe."

With Chloe on one side and Anna on the other, the three of them eased out onto the icy pond. Anna stopped a short way in. Her fear was easy to read.

"Everything will be okay, I promise," he assured her. "Trust me." He'd let Adam down all those years ago. He wasn't about to let the same thing happen to Anna. He'd protect her with his life if need be.

With her gaze locked onto his face, she slowly came toward him.

Chloe let go of his hand and skated away. Noah was surprised at how adept Chloe was for such a young age. He hadn't started skating until he was a bit older than she. But Chloe was a natural as she glided across the ice. Joseph had taught her well. Thinking of all the things Joseph was missing hurt. Noah wished his brother could be here with them now. He would so enjoy watching Chloe.

He glanced back to see Anna wobbling on her skates. "Steady now." Noah edged closer.

She managed a smile. "I'm a bit rusty, I guess."

He took her hand and slowed his pace.

"You're doing great." They slowly made their way around the small pond.

"When was the last time you went skating?" Noah asked, even though he knew.

She ducked her head, not looking at him. "Not in a long time."

"Not since Adam's death." He might as well say it, this thing that was between them, even though she didn't know the whole story.

"I know I'm being silly. It was an accident, but I can't help the way I feel. Skating claimed my brother's life. I never understood how Joseph could enjoy the activity after what happened to Adam, and then to him as a result."

Noah froze. Joseph had taken on his blame and he still couldn't understand why.

She watched Chloe skim across the pond as if it were nothing at all. "He always took Chloe skating, and he never let the past get to him."

Noah tamped down his guilt. "That was Joseph. He had a way of living above his feelings. But I understand how you feel. I haven't been skating since then either. Maybe together, we can help each other heal."

Anna's slight smile melted his heart. "I'd like that."

He smiled back, and they continued around the pond.

She brushed an escaping strand of hair from her eyes. "Even when Joseph was going through the shunning, he was always so positive. He made his amends and worked hard to be accepted again by the community." She glanced his way. "You know how difficult things are for someone shunned."

He understood the reason for the shunning, and that the act wasn't about punishment as much as keeping peace in the community. Still, the hardship for the shunned person and the person's family made getting by a struggle.

"I'm sorry that happened to Joseph . . . and to you." Neither of them had deserved the punishment. Not for something Joseph wasn't responsible for.

"What happened no longer matters. I just wish he were still here. I miss him so much."

Her words were a bitter reminder of the love she still carried for Joseph. Would there ever come a time when she was ready to move on? And why was that suddenly so important to him?

9

Anna still held Noah's hand, and she didn't want to let him go. She felt safe with him. More than ever, she wished she could peek into his mind and see what was troubling him.

Even though facing the reminders of how she'd lost her brother was hard, she had looked forward to their skating trip to Emerson's Pond. Each moment she spent in Noah's company left her with a breathless feeling inside. She hadn't felt this way since she and Joseph were courting.

Since Jessie's visit, Anna hadn't been able to get her friend's warning out of her head. *He's not one of us, Anna. He won't be the person you need him to be.*

Her head knew all this, and yet there were moments when she'd catch him watching her, and sense would flee. Then when they were apart, she found herself guarding her heart against the inevitable pain to come. She shouldn't care for Noah, yet every time they were together, she forgot that.

"What are you so troubled about?" he asked.

She hated that her face gave so much away. She thought about it too much and stumbled.

He reached out and caught her around the waist. Their eyes met and she saw the same uncertainty she felt reflected in his.

She could feel the color warming her cheeks. She was behaving foolishly, imagining things that could never be. She had Chloe and Mercy. Her life was good. She shouldn't ask for more.

Anna pulled away and he let her go. "I think we should take a break. Chloe, come have some of your Grossmammi's hot chocolate to warm you up." Her voice sounded breathless, even to her own ears.

"Aw, Mamm," Chloe protested.

"Now Chloe, mind your Mamm," Noah scolded gently.

"Ja, Onkel Noah." Chloe skated to join Anna at the edge of the pond.

Anna took out the thermos and handed her daughter a cup of the warm liquid, then poured one for Noah. She sat on the bench and thought about the last time she and Joseph had been to Emerson's Pond. She'd sat on this same bench and watched her husband and daughter. Joseph understood her reluctance to go out on the ice—somehow he'd overcome his own—and he'd never pressured her.

Her brother was barely sixteen when he and Joseph had gone ice-skating on the river near her parents' home—against her Mamm's warning that the ice was melting quickly. Adam had fallen through and been swept under the ice by the river's current. He'd gone from a fun-loving teenage boy with his whole life ahead of him to a heartbreaking memory in a matter of minutes.

"Anna?" Her head jerked toward the sound of Noah's voice. She hadn't realized he was sitting next to her until he'd spoken. The tenderness on his face warmed her inside and made her wish, again, for things that were not possible.

She forced a smile. "I'm all right." She'd been happy until she allowed herself to remember—really remember—that tragic day Adam had died. The past had no place in this beautiful day.

He returned her smile, and the intensity in his eyes sent her heart hammering against her chest.

Noah squinted up at the perfect afternoon sky dotted with gathering clouds. "We should enjoy the rest of our skating before it grows dark."

"You're right."

Chloe finished the last of her chocolate and set down the cup. "Come skate with me, Mamm."

Anna laughed and clasped her daughter's hand. "That sounds like a wonderful idea. Let's go." Together they skated out onto the pond and began making figure eights as Anna remembered her old skill. Noah watched them from the bench and Anna tried not to sneak little glances his way.

Soon, Noah set down his cup and joined them. He moved with an ease she would never be able to accomplish. The three of them skated around the pond together, and Anna couldn't keep from comparing this day to the last one she and Joseph had spent here before his death. If only she had known back then that their skating trip would be the last time they were together as a family, she would have clung to each moment, maybe even tried skating herself so as to be nearer to him. Like today, that time had been picture-perfect. Joseph had told her she was beautiful and the best wife he could have asked for. She'd loved him so much.

As hard as it was to let that day go, for Chloe's sake she couldn't stay in the past with all its sadness too long. Her daughter needed her to be strong and help her move forward. The days that were coming without Henry in her life were going to be difficult for Chloe. Soon, the spring planting would be upon them, and Noah would be gone as well. Once he hired the helpers needed, he would leave, and their life would return to normal. But it would be hollow without him. She would miss him terribly.

Anna shook herself and focused on her daughter's laughter. No sense letting things she couldn't change ruin the day.

With the setting sun, the sky became brilliant with shades of pink and orange.

"We should probably head home before darkness sets in," Noah said with clear reluctance.

Anna nodded. He was right, even though she hated to see their time come to an end.

"Can we stay a little longer, Onkel Noah? Please?" Chloe pleaded.

Noah glanced down into Chloe's sweet face and gave in. "Only for a little while, and then we must head home. You need your rest. You're spending the day with Grossmammi tomorrow while your Mamm goes to work."

Chloe squealed with glee.

While Noah and Chloe glided back and forth across the pond, Anna removed her skates and carried them and the hot chocolate to the buggy.

Chloe waved at her, her tiny face lit up with happiness. Guilt tugged at Anna's heart. She had been so busy surviving the last year that she had not always been the mother she wanted to be, the mother that Chloe deserved.

She gave them a few more minutes, then called, "Time to go, Chloe, before the temperature drops even more."

Noah and Chloe slowly made their way to the bench. Noah knelt in front of his niece and helped Chloe remove her skates.

"This has been a nice day," he said. There was a sadness in his voice. "I'll remember it always."

Anna felt the same way. "Danki for bringing us."

He bowed his head. "You are welcome. I'm glad I came. To be honest with you, I wasn't so sure I could do it. But now, I'm grateful."

She knew exactly what he meant. Being back on the ice and not remembering Adam's tragic death had been impossible, but by doing so, they'd reclaimed the joy of skating again.

Noah took Chloe's hand, and together they went to the buggy.

Noah turned Esther toward Anna's house. Like him, she would remember this day, no matter what the future held.

Noah sneaked a peek. Anna seemed to be deep in thought, a tiny smile lifting the corners of her mouth. Did she have any idea how pretty she was with her cheeks pink from the cold and the wind blowing wisps of hair across her face?

He would have given anything to know what she was thinking. Had she enjoyed the day as much as he? Noah believed she did. He couldn't remember a happier day, despite the dark memories it had dredged up. Today had been a blessing, and all because of the two people seated next to him.

She caught him watching her, and so he focused on the road in front of them. He could feel heat creeping up his neck. His feelings for Anna had been changing since he'd returned to Rexford. He'd need to find a way to distance himself if he didn't want to lose his heart.

Once they reached Anna's home, Noah lifted a sleeping Chloe and carried her inside while Anna climbed down on her own. He didn't offer his hand. He was feeling too vulnerable.

The broken window didn't sit well with him. Sure, an animal trying to gain access could be responsible for the incident, but in light of everything else, there could be a more dangerous explanation.

"I'll go get the board for the window." He headed toward the barn without waiting for her answer.

He found a board of about the right size and the can of nails he'd left there after one of his home repair projects, then returned to the house.

"Would you like to stay for dinner?" Anna asked from the kitchen.

He wanted to be able to tell her yes, ached to belong here with her and Chloe. But he didn't. "I should get back home."

"Please, Onkel Noah," Chloe protested sleepily. "I don't want you to go yet."

Rejecting the offer was next to impossible, but he had no choice. "Not today, dear one," he said, hating that he had to let the little girl down. He was starting to feel a little too at home with them. He had to keep reminding himself that this life wasn't his. Chloe wasn't his. Anna definitely wasn't his.

After he nailed up the board, he stepped into the kitchen so Chloe wouldn't hear his concerns. "I think you and Chloe should stay with my mother for a while. Until we know for sure what happened to the window."

Anna shook her head, her reaction not unexpected. "We'll be fine on our own. There's no need for worry. I'm sure it was just an animal, and you've taken care of that." Her tone implied she was hurt. Over what? Surely she didn't care whether he stayed for dinner.

"Anna—" he tried to argue, frustrated with her answer.

She turned away and called, "Chloe, I need you to help prepare the meal. Say goodbye to your Onkel."

He blew out a breath and hugged the little girl tight, trying to ignore the tears in her eyes.

"Are you coming tomorrow?" Chloe asked, her face scrunched up.

"We still have plenty of work to do around here, don't we?" he asked, delighted in spite of himself when Chloe's face lit up.

Noah glanced up to see Anna watching them. "If you don't mind, I'd like to take you to work tomorrow afternoon. I will start preparing the plowing equipment, and then come get you and Chloe. After what happened before, you can't be too careful. After you're done working,

I'll pick her up at Mamm's, and she and I can start to work on that squeaky door." He winked at Chloe.

"That's very kind of you, but not necessary. I will be fine."

"I want to," he told her, and he didn't give her time to say no. "Good night, Anna. I will see you tomorrow."

He turned on his heel, opened the door, and headed for the buggy without realizing Anna had followed him out.

"Noah, wait," she called after him.

He stopped halfway down the steps and slowly turned to face her.

"Is everything oke?" she asked, confusion clear on her face.

The day had been emotional, filled with some difficult memories. He needed time alone. At least, that's what he told himself. He couldn't admit that he just needed to get away from her before he lost his heart completely.

He didn't want to frighten her, but she needed to know his suspicions. "I'm worried, Anna. What if the window wasn't just an animal and someone was trying to break in? They could be back. I wish you'd come to the house with me."

Her brave smile didn't fool him. "Who would want to break into my home? We'll be oke. Good night, Noah."

He accepted her answer reluctantly and stepped up into the buggy, then turned Esther back to the road leading to the Millers' place.

He'd brought some of the tools from his life as a spy with him, careful not to let his Mamm or Anna see them. He wanted to take another good look at the equipment that was being set up there. Tomorrow, after he was able to size up Edward Latham's character, he'd call Robert and ask him to check on both the Latham and the Miller properties. There couldn't be that many vehicles like that SUV at the Lathams' place in Rexford.

As he eased Esther along the road rutted by heavy equipment, he wondered why his Mamm had never mentioned the place being sold. He'd ask her about it tomorrow.

Noah stopped Esther a little way from the entrance in a spot obscured by trees, then jumped down and grabbed his gear. As he eased toward the fence, the noise of heavy equipment running came from the property. He slipped closer and watched. This evening, the place was crawling with activity. He'd come here to check out the area where his brother had fallen to his death. With all the noise going on around the place, he should be able to slip into the location without anyone suspecting a thing.

He tied Esther to a tree out of sight from the activity, then climbed the fence, his earlier compunctions about trespassing gone. It was high time he got some answers. From what he could tell, the men were in the middle of clearing trees from the property. What was really going on here?

Keeping in the shadows as much as possible, Noah made his way to the back side of the property, where Joseph had fallen.

He hadn't been here since he was a teen, when he and Joseph would come help the elderly Miller family from time to time. The couple didn't have any children of their own, so Henry had watched out for them. Mercy had told him when Mr. Miller passed away a few years earlier, and Joseph and Henry had continued to work the farm for Mrs. Miller. Then, according to Anna, his Daed and brother had decided to buy the property. Since then, Mrs. Miller was now deceased as well. Had she sold the property to someone else before her death?

Noah stared into the dark abyss. Seeing the spot where his brother had lost his life ripped at his heart. He brought out his flashlight and aimed the light down the ten-foot drop. A frown creased his face as he surveyed where the accident had taken place. It didn't add up. Joseph was an expert at handling horses—he'd been doing so since he was a child. So how had he plunged off the side of the cliff? Even if he had, the drop was survivable, as long as he hadn't hit his head on a rock. And more importantly, why had he been so close to the edge? Joseph would never put a horse in jeopardy, much less himself.

Something below, near the property line, caught his attention. What appeared to be a dozen or more barrels were lying around. What did they contain?

He shook his head. Something was wrong here. Maybe he was grasping at straws to explain the accidents piling up on his family, but he didn't think so.

"Hey, do you see that light back there? Looks like someone's trespassing," a man yelled behind him. It was time to leave.

He quickly extinguished the flashlight and slipped back into the woods close by.

Once the forest concealed him, Noah hid behind a tree and watched. Half a dozen men appeared in the cleared area near the drop-off, several holding flashlights. They searched the place where Noah had been. He flattened himself behind the pine tree when one of the flashlight's beams came too close.

"I don't see anything. I'm guessing the noise was coming from the Amish farm next door and you only thought you saw a light. Come on, we have work to do. You know the boss wants this place cleared as quickly as possible so that we can be up and running soon. We still have other properties to clear. Everything hinges on them being functional when he buys that final piece of land."

After sweeping their flashlight beams around for a few more minutes, the men trudged away. Once Noah was positive they were gone, he headed back toward the buggy.

Something ugly was going on here. As he neared the office area, he heard a heated argument taking place. He moved as close as he dared to listen.

One man stood next to the driver's door of a massive SUV. The second man was blocked from sight by the vehicle, but Noah recognized the SUV right away. Latham had been driving the same vehicle at Anna's home earlier. Noah brought out his phone and typed in the license plate number.

"I told you this would happen if we didn't convince the old man to sell somehow. But you chose to use force instead, and look where that ended up. We need that land. Everything else is useless without it."

"I have things under control. I'll handle this," the hidden man snapped, not bothering to hide his anger.

"You'd better. Because if you can't get the job done, then what good are you to me? And you know what happens to people who are no good to me." The warning hung uncomfortably between the men.

The man he could see went back into the portable office building. After a second, the man hidden by the SUV climbed inside, backed the vehicle out, and headed off the property.

Noah's senses were on high alert. Who had he been talking about, and what were these men up to? Whatever was in the works here couldn't wait until tomorrow. He needed to speak to his coworker at the CIA now.

Once Noah reached the buggy, he noticed the SUV heading toward the Latham ranch. This wasn't a coincidence.

He eased the buggy around and put much-needed space between himself and what was happening at the Millers' place. When he was a safe distance away, he retrieved his cell phone and called his friend.

"Hey, buddy, good to hear from you. Is your family okay?" Robert knew about his father's passing.

"Things are okay, I guess. I'm surviving it." Noah swallowed back the lump in his throat. He still couldn't believe his Daed was gone.

"I get it. Losing your dad is hard. I still miss mine. How long are you going to be away? We sure could use you on this latest assignment."

Even with darkness surrounding him, the tranquility of the place he'd once called home settled around him. How would he ever manage to leave this peaceful place again for the dangers and unending stress of his job with the CIA? He realized all of a sudden that he was exhausted down to his bones at the very idea.

"I'm not sure. I still need to make sure my Ma—my mother is taken care of." Robert wouldn't understand the word for "mother" in the language Noah had grown up with. Robert wouldn't understand a lot of things about Noah's heart and what he longed for from his life now. He took a breath before getting to the reason for his call. "Listen, I need you to run a license plate and see who owns the vehicle. The plate's from Montana, probably from near Eureka." Noah gave him the number.

Robert was clearly surprised. "Montana? Is that where you're from? I had no idea."

Noah cleared his throat and debated how much to tell. "Yes, I grew up near here. Anyway, can you check on the plate for me?"

"Sure thing. I'll get started on it right away. What has you interested in this vehicle all of a sudden?"

Noah wasn't ready to tell his friend his reasons yet. "I just get the sense that something's not on the up and up with the owner. Can you leave me a message when you have something? And Robert, I need you to check on an Edward Latham as well. Same area."

"You think he's connected to the plate somehow?"

Noah wondered the same thing. From what Anna told him, the man had been a rancher all his life. He didn't understand why

Latham would be part of something shady. Still, his odd behavior earlier was troubling—and he'd been driving the same SUV Noah had just seen here.

"Let's just say he's a person of interest. I'd appreciate any help you can give me." He remembered the Miller farm. "Also, do you mind checking on the sale of some property around this area? The Miller family once owned the place. And check on sales of farms abutting the Millers too." Noah told him what he knew so far.

Robert chuckled. "No problem. I'll check on them and let you know something by tomorrow for sure. In the meantime, is there anything else I can do for you?"

Robert was a good friend and had Noah's back through some of the most dangerous missions he had ever worked. He trusted Robert with his life, but he wasn't ready to expose his assumptions just yet.

"Not at the moment. I appreciate the help, though, and I'll check in with you in a few days."

Once he'd ended the call, he made the rest of the trip home, uneasy the whole way. He had a feeling the truth behind both his father's and brother's deaths was going to be hard to accept.

Help me, he prayed. Whether or not he was ready to hear the truth, it needed to be known. But right now, Noah was in desperate need of something good to remember. As always, Anna's smiling face came to mind. The way she'd blushed so prettily whenever his hand touched hers made him believe she felt something for him as well. As hard as he tried, he couldn't deny that his feelings for Anna had changed—into something that could be just as dangerous for his heart as his job was for his life.

10

A fresh inch of snow clung to everything. Anna usually loved the winters here in the mountains, where the beauty of the frosted world around her made her want to be a child again. But this year, spring couldn't get here fast enough.

Then she remembered that spring this year meant Noah would leave again. Maybe winter could stick around a little longer.

As if she'd read her mind, Chloe asked, "Mamm, can we go see Onkel Noah today?"

She saw the sadness in her Dochder's eyes, and her heart went out to the child. Chloe had watched Noah pass by earlier that morning and wanted to go with him, but Anna knew how much work lay ahead for him. Soon the frost would be out of the ground and it would be time for plowing. She was grateful to Noah for making sure the equipment was ready.

"Oh, I don't know. Your Onkel is awfully busy this morning."

"Please? I miss him."

Anna felt herself wavering a bit. She missed him too. What could it hurt to stop by for a little while?

"I have an idea. Why don't we take him lunch? We'll stay for the meal, and then you'll go to Grossmammi's, and I'll come home and get ready for work later today."

Chloe clapped her hands with joy.

Anna retrieved a basket and tried to dismiss the warnings going off in her head. Her feelings for Noah were deepening. But try as she might, she couldn't see a happy ending for them.

"Get your cloak." Anna put the sauerbraten she'd prepared for lunch into the basket and slid on her own cloak before tying on her traveling bonnet. Her gaze flicked to the repaired window near the door. With no further incidents, Anna was inclined to believe that the window had been broken by a wild animal seeking warmth.

She and Chloe walked out to the barn. Once Anna harnessed Marta, she put the basket on the seat and lifted Chloe up.

"Mind the basket," she said as they headed to the outbuilding where the plowing and harvesting equipment was housed, about halfway between her own house and her mother-in-law's.

"There he is!" Chloe exclaimed, pointing.

Noah must have spotted them as well because he headed their way, waving and smiling. He seemed genuinely happy to see them.

As they drew closer, Anna's heart raced at the sight of him. *Stop it. He's leaving.*

"This is a nice surprise," he said, once they'd stopped the buggy.

Chloe clambered down and ran into his arms. He held her close. Over the child's head, Noah's gaze tangled with Anna's, and her chest grew tight. She'd never thought she could love again, and yet she was falling hard for him.

"We thought we'd bring you lunch, if you can take a break," she said by way of explanation.

He took the basket from her. "That sounds nice."

Anna had to look away from the intensity in his eyes.

"Come into the shelter of the barn," he said. "I have a fire going." He quickly set up a makeshift table and benches near the stove and Anna began to lay out the meal.

"Sauerbraten?" His eyes lit up. "This happens to be one of my favorites, and I haven't had it in a very long time." As he helped her with dishes and silverware, his hand brushed against hers. Their eyes met again, but this time she didn't avoid his gaze. It was probably futile—wrong, even—but a small part of her wanted him to know how she felt about him, just this once.

Noah smiled, and her heart longed for it to be a promise never to leave her. Why did she yearn for the impossible?

He sampled the sauerbraten and closed his eyes. "Delicious. I know this takes days to marinate before it's braised. You've grown up from that freckle-faced little girl who used to follow Adam and me around all those years ago and try to serve us pretend cookies and pies made of grass and mud."

The warmth in his eyes as they swept over her face made normal breathing impossible. Anna's gaze fell to her plate and she tried to steady her crazy heartbeat.

Chloe giggled at her uncle's description. "My Mamm wasn't ever a little girl."

In spite of the awkwardness, Anna joined in her daughter's amusement.

"Oh yes, she was," Noah confirmed. As he continued to stare at Anna, the smile left his face and something she couldn't name replaced it.

She wondered what her own face showed him.

Noah cleared his throat. "I'm almost finished here for the day. I'll take the horses home, then come back and collect you and Chloe," he said with a catch in his voice.

Anna studied the still-frozen field outside, trying to reclaim her composure. "Are you sure you want to stop what you're doing to take me to work? I know you're busy here."

Noah touched her hand, pulling her gaze from the field toward him like a magnet. "I want to come with you, Anna. I don't understand what Latham is up to, and until I'm sure, I don't want you going there without me."

"Why would you think he was up to something? He's a sweet old man." She gathered the leftovers and placed the food in the basket.

"Just a feeling, I guess." Noah rose to his feet and held out his hand to help her up, and Anna let him pull her to her feet.

She circled to her daughter. "Say goodbye to your Onkel, Chloe. We need to let him finish his work, and I have chores to do at the house."

"But Mamm," Chloe whined.

Noah winked at his niece. "Be nice to your mother. She let you come here today, didn't she?"

They waved to Noah and were on their way. Once they reached the house, Anna put away the leftover food and finished up a few chores.

An hour later, a buggy headed their way. Noah. Anna kept remembering what he'd said to her at their lunch. Could he possibly care for her? She shook her head. He had a way of occupying far too much of her thoughts.

"Chloe, finish your snack. We need to go. Your Onkel is here."

Chloe popped the last bite of her apple fry pie into her mouth and ran to the door. Before Anna could stop her, she pulled the door open and rushed outside.

"Chloe, wait." Anna ran after her daughter who had cleared the steps and was waiting for Noah to jump down from the buggy, dancing in place.

He climbed down and scooped Chloe up into his arms and swung her around. The same happiness reflected on her daughter's face was there on his, melting Anna's heart.

"Is that fry pie I see right here? Didn't you get enough lunch?" He brushed a crumb from the side of Chloe's mouth, and she giggled. Anna loved the sound of it. Since Noah's return, her daughter was happier than she'd been in a long time.

She nodded eagerly. "Can I come with you and Mamm to her work today?"

Over the top of the child's head, his eyes met Anna's and she shook her head. Chloe had asked her that same question half a dozen times since she'd overheard Noah talking about taking Anna to work.

"Not this time. Your Mamm has work to do, and she's still not completely healed."

"But you get to go. That's not fair." Chloe was not usually a child who pouted, but she was doing it now.

"Chloe, your Onkel is only driving me because of my injury," Anna explained. "I'm going there to work. Besides, your Grossmammi would miss you if you weren't there to keep her company today. Now, go get your doll and your coat so we can go."

Noah set the child down, but Chloe didn't move. "Do as your Mamm asks," he said, his voice gentle but firm.

A willful Chloe trudged past Anna into the house, and Anna suppressed a laugh.

In so many ways, her daughter reminded Anna of herself at that age. She'd been stubborn beyond belief. She remembered how patient her own Mamm had been with her. Her Daed as well, although he had had a firm hand when needed for both her and Adam.

"She takes after me, I'm afraid. She has a mind of her own," Anna said while they waited for Chloe to return.

"Oh, I remember all too well." A grin formed on his face. "You used to get so mad at Adam and me when we didn't let you come with us."

She started to disagree, but she couldn't because he was right. Most of the time Adam and Noah had been patient with her and let her tag along wherever they went, but there were times when they wanted to do boy things like hunt and build forts. Her Mamm and

Daed would encourage her to stay home, but she'd sneak out of the house and hunt them down.

"That's because I liked hanging out with you two. You always did such fun things, and I wanted to join in." Truth be told, her ten-year-old heart had developed a huge crush on Noah by then. That was part of the reason why she followed them around so much.

He stepped closer, and she didn't know whether she wanted to close the distance even more or put the proper space between them. His brilliant blue eyes held hers. "Anna . . ." Before he could say anything else, Chloe raced from the house, breaking the spell.

Anna would have given anything to know what he had been about to say.

"Ready?" he asked Chloe. When she nodded, his gaze returned to Anna. "If you want, I can drive you into town later to take your finished quilt to Mrs. Schwartz. I'd like to see if she would be willing to put up some flyers for hiring workers to do the planting."

Anna could only nod as her heart splintered. She hurried to retrieve the quilt, her breath hanging in her throat at the look in his eyes as he took it from her.

She followed Noah and her daughter to the buggy. When their hands touched, that familiar tingle shot through her, but she shoved it down.

Noah turned the buggy around and they headed back to Mercy's place. He surely didn't understand the sudden change in her—if he even noticed it—and she couldn't disclose to him how she felt. She couldn't keep him here against his will. She couldn't ask him to give up the life he wanted for her.

"Everything okay?" he asked after they had dropped off Chloe.

Anna hadn't spoken the whole ride. She cleared her throat and braced herself to face him again. She dug deep and managed a smile.

"Everything is fine. I'm just thinking about what needs to be done at the Lathams' today."

He nodded and she focused straight ahead once more. He was still planning to leave. Had it all been just her imagination, or had he felt something when they were together?

Even though Anna claimed nothing was wrong, Noah knew that wasn't the truth. And it probably had something to do with him. He'd pulled back from her, and she probably sensed that. His feelings were only going to get them both hurt.

Instead of conversation, his thoughts reverted to the SUV at the Millers' place the evening before, which he'd bet was the same one that Latham had gotten into at Anna's house. He didn't like the connection one bit, and until he figured out what was going on, he didn't plan on leaving Anna alone with Latham.

When it was the two of them again, after they dropped off Chloe, he struggled to find a way to ask her about Latham without worrying her. Noah had searched his memory, but he didn't remember the Lathams from when he was a kid.

"How long have the Lathams lived in the area?" He kept his attention straight ahead, hoping to keep his suspicions to himself, though she already knew he had concerns.

Anna moved in her seat. He could feel her watching him. She had always been good at reading him, even as a child. He remembered all those times when he was younger, and he and Adam would try to slip away from Anna. She'd find them easily enough simply because she'd seen something in his eyes.

"About seven years or so, I guess. Noah, why are you so worried about Edward?"

While he hesitated, unsure of how much to tell her of his suspicions, she guessed the truth.

"You think he was involved in my accident." It wasn't a question.

He still couldn't think of how to answer.

"There's more to it, isn't there? Noah, tell me what's going on."

As much as he didn't want to worry her, she deserved to know the truth.

"That vehicle that your employer drove the other day—I saw it at the Miller place last night."

He peered over at her and could tell she was struggling to understand.

"What were you doing at the Miller place?"

He answered her question with one of his own. "Did you know the place had been sold?"

Her eyes grew wide. "I had no idea."

"Someone bought the property, and they've moved in a lot of heavy equipment."

"Really?" Her forehead furrowed. "I've heard a lot of noise coming from that way, but I haven't been back to the place since . . ." She didn't finish, but he understood.

"Anyway, I noticed the SUV that Latham drove to your house parked in front of a portable building the new owner installed there. They are probably planning to use the building as an office."

There was too much apprehension in her eyes. "Why were *you* there, Noah?"

He blew out a sigh. "I went there to check out the place where Joseph fell."

"Why would you do that?" Her words sounded choked.

"Because something about it didn't add up in my head. Joseph was an expert rider. There's no way he would deliberately put himself or his horse in danger, and the fall wouldn't have been enough to kill him. I don't think his death was an accident."

Her wide eyes filled with shock. "And you think Edward is somehow responsible? He's like a father to me. He would never do anything to hurt me or anyone else."

That was the part that didn't add up in his mind. Anna clearly loved the man and his wife, and he'd have said she was an excellent judge of character. But how well did she really know them?

"I'm not saying he's involved. I'm simply being careful. I don't want anything to happen to you again."

She gave him a sad smile. Anna was a kind and gentle soul, and his heart ached to call her his.

"To be safe, I'll stay outside until you're finished. Maybe I can get a handle on what's going on here by talking to Latham."

"All right, but don't interrogate him. He's been nothing but kind to me."

He nodded, and they entered the Lathams' gate. Noah slowed the mare to a halt in front of the ranch house.

Once he'd helped her down, he accompanied her to the door.

"I'll introduce myself, and then I can hang out with Esther until you're ready to leave. Maybe do a little poking around. If you need anything, I'll be right out here."

Anna knocked, then waited while seconds passed. The door opened, and Edward stood before them.

The first impression Noah had was of a kind-looking older man who couldn't hurt anyone. But when he studied the other man, he could see that the man appeared to be struggling with his own demons. He was as pale as a sheet, and there were dark circles under his eyes, as if he hadn't slept in days.

"Anna, I'm so glad to see you." Edward reached over and hugged her, clearly shocking Anna by the gesture.

After a moment, she pulled away, a blush spreading across her cheeks.

"And you've brought someone with you." He seemed to be sizing up Noah.

"Yes, this is Noah Petersheim, my brother-in-law. He gave me a ride."

Edward stuck out his hand. "Thank you for helping Anna. Welcome to my home." He turned to Anna. "You shouldn't exert yourself too much. I would hate for you to have a setback."

Next to him, Anna froze at the man's choice of words, yet Latham's expression was innocent enough. *Great, now I've got her all paranoid like me.*

"Noah, why don't I show you around the place while Anna goes about her chores?"

Noah was hoping to have a chance to look around the ranch, and now he was being offered a guided tour. It was almost too good to be true. *Maybe it is.*

Anna headed inside.

Latham stepped out and closed the door. "Let's start with the barn there. I have some vintage tractors I'm quite proud of."

As they headed to the barn Latham had pointed out, Noah surveyed the surrounding area. Nothing set off any warning signs. Beyond the SUV, why was he so suspicious of this man?

The barn contained half a dozen different antique tractors, all restored to their former glory. In one corner, a vehicle was covered by a tarp.

Latham was explaining the different types of tractors when he received a call. Noah could tell the other man wasn't happy to see the name of the caller on his phone.

"Will you excuse me a moment?"

Noah studied the man's nervous reaction before nodding. Latham didn't answer the call until he was outside, and then he put several feet between himself and the barn before continuing the conversation.

Noah couldn't make out what was said, so he hurried toward the tarp and lifted it up. Under it he found the SUV from the previous day. Noah brought out his cell phone and compared the license plate number to the one he'd seen at the Millers' place to confirm. They matched. He examined the front of the vehicle. There were definite signs of damage there. This was the vehicle that had run Anna off the road.

Had Edward Latham had anything to do with his brother's and father's deaths as well?

11

Noah was quiet on the ride back to Mercy's, and Anna was afraid he wasn't telling her something.

"What's wrong?" she finally asked.

He hesitated, then took a deep breath and said, "I found the vehicle that ran you off the road. The SUV is the same one that Latham drove to your house. It was also at the Millers' place yesterday, only he wasn't driving it then. Anna, I don't think you should go back there until we know how involved he is with everything that's happened."

"There's no way he had anything to do with my accident."

He covered her hand with his. The warmth she felt with their hands entwined sent her heart soaring. She tried to tamp the feeling down.

"Let's hope not. Maybe this will all prove to be some strange coincidence."

She could tell he didn't believe that.

Once they reached Mercy's house, they both climbed down. Anna made sure she was on the ground before he could help her.

"I'll be right there," Noah said. "I need to take care of something first."

She sensed that something was troubling him, more than he'd chosen to share with her. "What?"

"It's nothing. I've just asked my friend with the CIA to check up on who bought the Millers' place and to do a little research on Latham. There's a connection there that I don't understand, and I believe it will reveal who really killed Joseph and my father."

Shock rooted her in place. "You think both Joseph's and Henry's deaths were murders? Why? Why would someone want to harm either of them?"

He shook his head. "I don't know. I hope to have some answers soon."

He hurried into the barn without another word. He was doing everything in his power to find out what was going on. She needed to do her part and make sure Mercy and Chloe didn't worry.

She went inside the house and closed the door.

"There you are, Anna. Where's Noah?" Mercy asked.

"He's coming. He needed to take care of something first." She did her best to sound reassuring.

"Mamm." Chloe ran into Anna's open arms. "We made dinner for you." Her daughter smiled and pointed to the table, which was set.

"You did?" Anna made a great show of inhaling deeply. "Whatever you made smells wonderful."

Chloe clasped her hand and led her to the table. "We made your favorite."

She spotted the pork potpie and hugged Mercy close. "Danki."

Mercy waved her hands in front of her. "Ach, it was nothing. I wanted to do something nice for you. You've been working so hard to keep our households going."

Anna clutched Mercy's hand tightly. "I wish there was more that I could do."

"You do more than you should have to." A frown flickered over Mercy's face. "I wish—" She didn't finish, but Anna knew. Mercy so wished Noah were home to stay this time. Anna didn't have the heart to tell her about Noah's request to go with her to Mrs. Schwartz's store so he could post flyers for help.

She owed so much to this woman who had taken her into her family. Painful as it would be, they'd survive without Noah.

He came in a few minutes later and removed his coat. "What

smells so good?" He kissed his mother's cheek and peeked over her shoulder.

"I had lots of help today, thanks to Chloe. And we're anxious for you to have some, so sit."

Once they were seated around the table, they bowed their heads for the silent prayer, and for the fist time since he'd been home, Noah joined in. Anna couldn't help but see this as a sign, although her head told her to keep her heart guarded. He might simply be doing it out of respect.

"Tell us about your first day back at work," Mercy said.

"It was *gut*. There were no problems," she answered too quickly, and Mercy eyed her.

"I'll be taking Anna into town before dark to drop off her finished quilt. Do you need me to pick up anything for you?" Noah asked, taking the spotlight off Anna, much to her relief.

Mercy beamed at his thoughtfulness. "I can't think of a single thing."

Noah glanced down at his niece. "Do you want to come with us? We could stop by the bakery."

Chloe's eyes lit up. "Can I, Mamm?"

Anna automatically smiled and nodded, but all she could think about was how eager Noah was to post the flyers.

After the meal, Mercy shooed them off. "I can handle the cleanup. You three go and enjoy your trip."

During the ride into town, Anna was unable to think of a single thing to say, but she didn't have to. Chloe chattered on, happy to be going with them. Anna was too aware of Noah's presence, but she couldn't look at him.

He brought the buggy to a stop in front of the bulk goods store and retrieved the quilt Anna had packed. Once inside, he handed it to Mrs. Schwartz, whose eyes lit up when she saw it.

"Good to see you again, Anna, and you've brought your little one with you." Mrs. Schwartz reached inside the glass jar where she kept homemade hard candy and handed Chloe a piece.

"What do you say?" Anna prompted the girl.

"Danki," Chloe said obediently. She popped the candy into her mouth.

"I'll go put this quilt in the display case. And I have good news for you. We had a traveler from out of town stop by recently. He was asking about you. I think he might have known you. When I told him about your handmade quilts, he said he wanted to buy one for his wife."

Anna's gaze flew to Noah. Someone from out of town was asking about her? After everything that had happened recently, she couldn't believe this was a coincidence. From the look on his face, he didn't think so either. And he didn't like it any more than she did.

The next day, Noah peered down at the simple gravestone marking his Daed's burial site. Next to Henry, Joseph's marker reminded him of that somber day a year earlier. This was the first time he'd come here since he'd been home.

Tears welled up inside of him, and he wiped his eyes. He'd let his Daed down. After Joseph passed, he should have stayed on, knowing how difficult it would be for Henry to keep the place going, and yet he couldn't bear the memories. Still, no matter how far away from Rexford he ran, his part in Adam's death was always there beside him.

Everyone believed he'd left the community because he was grief-stricken, but that wasn't the whole truth. He had been there on the day Adam died.

The wind was bitterly cold that day, but that didn't stop the three teenage boys from planning to meet up and skate on the frozen river. Noah had to finish some extra chores for his Daed, so Joseph and Adam were already there when he arrived.

"What are you waiting for?" he asked. "I thought we were going to skate."

"My Mamm says the ice will be melting too quickly this time of year with the weather warming up and the current under the ice. It's too dangerous," Adam said. "I don't think we should."

Noah was irritated from working longer than his brother had to. He'd been looking forward to the skate, gliding along the ice and trying new tricks while joking and laughing with his brother and his best friend. And now Adam didn't want to do it at all?

"What, is Mamm's little boy scared?" he taunted.

Adam stiffened. "No, I'm just not stupid," he snapped.

"Are you saying I'm stupid?" Noah bellowed. Before he knew what he was doing, he gave his friend a strong, two-armed shove to the chest.

"Hey, stop!" Joseph protested.

The older boys ignored him.

"You're certainly acting stupid!" Adam roared back. He gave Noah an even harder push back.

Noah staggered back and tripped over a log on the river's edge. He landed on the ice.

There was a sickening crack.

What happened next was etched into Noah's mind for the rest of his life. He could play the scene in slow motion in his memory.

Adam's face morphed from rage to terror. "Noah!" he cried. Before *anyone could stop him, he lunged toward his friend and shoved him off the damaged ice.*

Noah spun away onto thicker ice. He stopped just in time to see the ice give way where he had just been.

Adam disappeared.

"Adam!" he and his brother screamed in unison.

Noah pushed himself to his feet and raced toward the hole, slipping and sliding, but his friend was gone, swept away under the ice by the current. He sprinted down the frozen river, Joseph running beside him along the bank, but he never saw Adam again.

Joseph came out onto the ice and grabbed his arm. "Noah, he's gone," he sobbed.

"No! Let go! We can still find him!"

"It's no use. And what if you fall through too?"

Joseph was right. Noah collapsed to the ice as the realization sank in that his best friend had just died saving his life. Someone was screaming Adam's name over and over in a terrible, hoarse voice.

It would be years before he realized that it was his own.

He alone was to blame.

Noah buried his face in his hands. "Daed, help me. What should I do?" he whispered, as he had asked his father's advice so many times growing up. He felt more lost now than he ever had as a child.

And just as if Henry had given his answer in his kind, simple way, what Noah needed to do became clear in a flash. The answer had always been there—he just didn't want to accept it because it was so hard for him to be in Rexford. His Mamm needed him now more than ever. She was putting on a brave front, but she was hurting. He thought about his niece. The little girl had taken to him from the start, and he loved her like she was his own child. And then there was Anna. He couldn't deny that his feelings for her had deepened, and that scared him.

He knew what his Daed would have him do, and he owed it to Henry to help make his Mamm's life easier.

Noah swallowed the lump in his throat. "Okay, I'll stay until the spring planting is finished. And by then I'll have found capable workers to take over the tending of the fields. I won't let Mamm and Anna fend for themselves."

The decision hadn't been an easy one, but when it was made, he felt a sense of peace settle around him. Staying for the planting was the right thing to do, and there was only one person he wanted to share his decision with—Anna.

As he headed back to the buggy, he spotted Adam's gravestone. After Adam's death, he hadn't attended the funeral service. He'd simply run away. He'd been running ever since.

He fell to his knees beside Adam's grave. "I'm so sorry, Adam. I shouldn't have teased you. You were right to be nervous about skating that day, and I should have just listened to you. I can never repay the debt I owe you."

The apology came far too late, but he wanted to say he was sorry just the same.

Noah still couldn't imagine what had possessed his brother to take on the blame for what he'd done all those years after Adam's death. And he still couldn't believe the bishop and elders had passed such strong punishment for what had been an accident.

He touched the gravestone gently. Adam's parents were laid to rest next to him. They'd died never knowing the truth behind their son's death. Anna still believed her husband had been the one responsible for her brother's death. He should set the record straight, yet every time he tried, he couldn't say the words and have her hate him for being a coward who'd abandoned his community and let his brother take the fall for his actions.

Noah headed back to the buggy. He'd promised Chloe he would stop by later that day so that they could do some work together. They'd finished up most of the repairs, yet he'd keep finding things to do if it meant he could be with Chloe and Anna.

He had just started toward her house when his phone rang. Noah pulled over the buggy and answered.

"Please tell me you have some news," he said.

The length of time it took Robert to answer did little to reassure him. "Well, I do, but not very much. I found out who bought the Miller place. It's a company by the name of Northern Montana Energy."

Noah stared at the mountains in the distance. "Northern Montana Energy?" He'd never heard of them. "What do they do?"

"They drill oil wells. Based on the heavy equipment you saw on the Miller property, I bet they're planning to test drill."

"Let me guess. They've also bought up some of the surrounding farmland."

"Bingo. The business is fairly new, but so far what I've found out is like peeling back an onion. There are more layers than I expected, and I haven't found the name of the owner yet."

Noah didn't like the sound of that. "How long have they been operating here in Montana?"

"Less than a year. They've bought at least six properties. Hundreds of acres."

"Someone has deep pockets. What about the vehicle? Did anything pan out there?"

"Just that the SUV is registered to Northern Montana Energy as well." Robert sighed his frustration. "On the other hand, I checked on your Edward Latham, and he appears squeaky clean. He and his wife have been married for nearly forty years. They moved to their current home near Eureka from Billings about seven years ago. They have one son, Edward Junior, better known as Eddie. He doesn't have much of a history beyond living off his father's money. And he seems to have disappeared off the face of the earth recently."

"That's strange. I wonder if that has something to do with Edward Senior."

"I'm not sure, but it seems highly doubtful. As far as I can tell, he's a good person. But I'll keep checking on Latham and on Northern Montana Energy. I'll let you know when I have something more."

"Thanks, Robert. I appreciate your help." Noah ended the call and tucked the phone inside his pocket. He couldn't accept that Latham wasn't somehow involved in what was happening with Northern Montana Energy. There was such a thing as being too clean. Something bad was going on in Rexford, and he needed to figure out what before there were any more "accidents."

12

Two weeks later, after a warm spell that confirmed that spring had indeed finally arrived, Anna decided to enlist Chloe's help in preparing their garden. Her Dochder loved playing outside, and while she helped her Mamm with clearing the ground, she was also distracted by every little thing.

But Anna didn't mind. She loved digging in the dirt, and seeing her daughter so happy was nice. A lot of it was due to Noah, as was her own happiness, much as she didn't want to admit it. It would only lead to more hurt when he left again.

Anna continued to dig up the earth with her hoe, perspiration dampening her brow. She wanted to plant a big garden this year to help with their food supply. Canning food to help get through next winter would go a long way toward easing her mind.

Once she'd finished digging up the plot of land that would be her garden, Anna sat on the porch and watched as Chloe played in the yard. Out of the corner of her eye, she noticed someone coming their way. Noah. She clenched her hands together in her lap and tried to calm herself. She was behaving foolishly. There could be nothing between them.

"Onkel Noah is here!" Chloe jumped up from where she'd been studying something in a tall clump of grass.

"I see." Anna tried to keep her voice steady.

Chloe barely waited until Noah brought the mare to a stop. "Onkel Noah, come see our garden!"

Noah hopped down from the buggy and scooped the little girl

up, planting a loud kiss on her cheek and making her giggle. "You've been working in the garden? Come show me." He set Chloe on her feet again and waited for Anna to join them.

Anna wiped her grimy hands on her apron and steadied herself before leaving the porch.

"How are you today?" he asked gently when she joined them. Did he feel the same stirrings that she did? Thinking about the future broke her heart.

She swallowed hard. "I'm *gut*. And you?"

"The same. I have lots to tell you when the time is right." He nodded toward Chloe, and she understood.

"Come on." The little girl clutched Noah's hand and tugged him along behind her. Anna had to smile at her daughter's enthusiasm.

Chloe dragged her uncle to the area they'd cleared that morning. "See?" Her face beamed with pride as she waited for his approval.

"Wow." Noah admired the simple overturned dirt as if it were the most amazing thing in the world. "You and your Mamm have been busy. What will you plant in this fine garden?"

Anna tried not to laugh at his serious expression, but she had to smile at how he made her daughter feel special. He made her feel special too.

"Lots of things. Carrots. Beans. Grapes."

Anna covered her mouth to keep from laughing. She started to correct her daughter by telling her that grapes grew on vines and not in a vegetable garden, but Noah stopped her.

"You're going to grow grapes? That's my favorite fruit. Maybe you can grow some for me."

Chloe's grinned up at him. "I will."

"*Gut*. That's one beautiful garden, Chloe. I can almost picture it with vegetables growing now."

Chloe nodded proudly, then went to examine a worm burrowing in the loose earth.

"Do you have all the seeds you need for the garden?" Noah asked once the little one was distracted.

Anna nodded. "Ja, I save them each year. We should start planting soon."

She loved the way his eyes lit up when he laughed. The way he cared for her daughter and made sure she had everything she needed. His handsome face was branded on her heart.

"I went to see my Daed and brother today." He faced her. "I came to a decision."

She held her breath. "You did?" *Please say you'll never leave again.*

"I'm going to stay here until the spring planting is finished. I can't trust that to anyone else. It's too important. Once the planting is finished, I'll make sure the wheat crop is in capable hands."

Not showing disappointment took everything inside of her. "That's wonderful news," she heard herself saying.

"My mother needs me, and I'm enjoying my time with Chloe—and you." As his gaze held hers, her heart hammered unsteadily.

"Me too." Her words sounded breathless to her own ears.

"Onkel Noah, are we going to start work soon?"

"Dear, Noah just arrived," Anna chided gently.

Chloe's eyes darted from Noah to her. Did she see what was happening between them? Anna hoped not. She didn't want to get Chloe's hopes up. There could be no future for her and Noah.

"I don't mind," he told her. Was his voice husky, or was it her imagination? "I think it's high time we started. What would you like to do today, Chloe?"

Chloe thought about it for a second. "Can we fix the floor in my room?"

Noah nodded. "Good choice. We don't want any critters trying to get in bed with you at night. Help me carry in the tools."

Chloe ran ahead, but Noah hung back for a moment. She could see he had a lot to say to her, but now was not the time.

Concentrating on Chloe's happy chatter as they repaired the loose boards in her room was hard. All he could think about was the moment outside that he and Anna had shared. As much as he tried to convince himself he was only there to take care of Anna and Chloe for his brother, his heart knew that wasn't the truth. Anna had a way of making him realize what was missing from his own life. Things he had never considered possible for himself, like a family of his own.

"Onkel Noah!" The frustration in Chloe's tone told him she'd been trying to get his attention for a long time.

"Sorry, love. I guess I was lost in thought. What did you say?"

"Mamm has lunch ready."

"We shouldn't keep your Mamm waiting, then."

Noah poured water into a basin and helped Chloe wash her hands, and then they both headed to the kitchen.

Anna was stirring something on the stove when he came up next to her and looked over her shoulder. Had her shoulders tightened at his presence?

She cleared her throat. "Chicken soup with dumplings." She held the wooden spoon up for him to taste.

"Yum. I can't wait." It was foolish to imagine small moments like this becoming part of his everyday life, but he did it anyway.

He could see his compliment pleased her. He took a seat at the table with Chloe while Anna ladled three bowls of soup and then brought some fresh sourdough bread from the oven.

Noah bowed his head. He'd been awkward with the prayers when he first returned home. Now, he found himself looking forward to those quiet times when he could talk with Gött.

When the prayer ended, Noah dug into the hearty soup and crusty bread. More and more, he found the plain ways calling him back. Still, he was torn between wanting to stay and going back on the run from memories and guilt that had dogged him since his return. Could he make peace with Adam's death and Joseph's false confession once and for all and find his own peace here?

Help me, Gött, he silently prayed.

"This is wonderful, Anna," he said, noticing that she watched him. "You are a better cook than even my Mamm. But if you tell her I said that, I will deny it."

She smiled at his teasing. "Your secret is safe with me."

He loved watching Anna smile. Her face lit up and made her seem almost carefree.

"Onkel Noah, are you coming to church with us again?" His niece innocently asked the question he'd known was coming. Chloe wanted him to be there for every part of her life, and he felt the same way.

"Chloe," Anna scolded.

Noah smiled at Anna and held her gaze. "No, it's okay, Anna. I've been thinking about it a lot, and yes, I would like to come to church with you tomorrow, Chloe. If your Mamm's okay with me tagging along."

Her eyes lit up. "I would like that very much."

He knew he shouldn't give in to his feelings so much, but he couldn't help it. He'd never felt this way before. Perhaps she was the reason he'd never gotten serious about any other woman.

Noah finished his soup and took his bowl to the sink to wash out.

"Leave it. I'll get it later," Anna told him.

"You prepared this delicious meal. The least I can do is help with the cleanup. Chloe, why don't you help me? Can you bring your bowl here, please?"

Chloe carried her bowl to Noah, then brought her Mamm's bowl over as well. Before long the table and the dishes were clean, the leftovers stored in the gas-powered refrigerator.

Noah glanced out the kitchen window. "I should be getting home. I'm going to finish up the last of the repairs to the barn this afternoon."

"Do you have to go?" Chloe asked.

He shared the sentiment, but he needed to put some space between himself and his growing feelings for Anna.

He debated about telling her what Robert had said. No, best to leave that for another day. There was no reason to scare her.

"I will see you both tomorrow." He gathered his tools by the door and then put on his jacket and headed out the door.

"Noah, wait." Anna turned to Chloe. "Stay here. I'll be right back." She put on her cloak and followed him outside.

He waited until the door was closed. "There's nothing to be worried about," he said, anticipating her question.

"You said you had something to talk to me about. What's going on?"

He had said that. They sat together on the porch swing.

Trying—and failing—to ignore her nearness and how natural it felt to sit here with her like this, he said, "You remember I asked one of my colleagues to check into Latham and the company that bought the Millers' old place. They're called Northern Montana Energy. My friend is still checking on them, but so far he hasn't come across the name of the owner yet. They're buying up property around the area, though."

Her eyes widened in shock. "How is this connected to Edward?" She shook her head. "I'm sorry, but I can't believe he would do anything illegal."

Noah would do whatever he could to protect her. "Until we know what's really going on, we can't afford to dismiss anything, including him."

13

Anna spent the rest of the afternoon listening to Chloe chatter on about Noah, and she couldn't help but feel guilty. After losing Joseph, she had never been able to imagine sharing her life with another man. She loved Joseph so much. But since Noah had come back into her life, things were different. Her feelings were changing with every moment they spent together, and she was so worried. She couldn't give her heart to him, knowing that one day he wouldn't be part of their lives.

"Mamm, do you think Onkel Noah will be here for my birthday?" Chloe innocently asked.

Chloe's birthday was in September. He'd told her he planned to stay until the spring planting was finished, which would be long before Chloe's birthday.

"I don't know, Kind. Your Onkel has his own life outside of our community. At some point, he will have to leave us."

Chloe's eyes filled. "But I don't want him to go."

Anna held her daughter while she cried, feeling helpless. Chloe was so attached to Noah. If Anna were being honest, she was more than a little attached herself.

"Hush now," she said, trying to soothe the girl. "Enjoy the time we have with him, and don't worry about the future." *Are those words for her or for me?*

A buggy approached outside, and Anna went to the window. Jessie and her daughters waved.

"Go wash up, Chloe. We have company. Jessie and the girls are here."

Chloe perked up a little and ran to splash water on her tearful face. Then they hurried outside together to greet their company.

"What a nice surprise. I wasn't expecting you today," Anna told Jessie as she hugged her friend tight. All five girls raced past her toward the house.

"They have so much energy. I thought an outing would do them good."

Anna smiled sympathetically. "I can understand. Come inside. Would you like some tea or Kaffe?"

Jessie removed her cloak and bonnet and hung them on the pegs. "Since when do you drink Kaffe?"

Anna laughed at her friend's expression. "Since Noah bought me a percolator. I actually enjoy a good cup of Kaffe now."

She could almost read all the things going through Jessie's head. "Well, Kaffe sounds good. Girls, settle down and don't make a mess of the house."

"Yes, Mamm!" they called in unison.

Anna barely kept her amusement to herself. "Chloe, why don't you all go into your room to play?"

Once the girls were gone, Anna removed the percolator from the cupboard and measured Kaffe into it, then poured in the water and put it on the stovetop. "I'm in awe of how you manage those girls. Then again, you always could put the fear of Gött into anyone with just a look."

Jessie chuckled. "That skill really comes in handy when dealing with five energetic Kinner."

Anna smiled at her friend. "I can imagine. Want something sweet to go with the coffee?"

"I shouldn't, but I would love one of your fry pies if you have any."

"You're in luck." Anna brought two out from the refrigerator and placed them in the oven to warm.

Jesse leaned forward, all business now. "Oke, enough stalling. Tell me what's going on between you and Noah Petersheim. And don't say nothing, because I'm not blind. I see the way you look at him."

Anna had known it was only a matter of time before Jessie would want to have a heart-to-heart. She had to admit it would be nice to talk out the complicated situation with someone she trusted.

She poured two cups of coffee and took out milk and sugar, buying herself a little time to get her thoughts in order. "Well, Noah's been helping out with some of the repairs around here."

Jessie stirred in milk and sugar. "Uh-huh. You forget I know you." She placed a gentle hand over Anna's. "Would it be so bad if something were to happen?"

Anna swallowed hard. "Yes, because he won't be here that long. He's leaving after the spring planting. I can't fall in love with him, Jessie. I can't."

Jessie squeezed her hand. "Sounds like you already have."

Anna gaped at her friend. Was she in love? She hadn't felt this way in so long. Noah made her feel special, but there was no future for them.

She stared at her hands. "Well, it doesn't matter."

"What if he feels the same way about you?"

Anna shook her head. "I don't know how he feels, but I do know that we can never be."

"You deserve to be happy, Anna. I know you loved Joseph, but he wouldn't want you to mourn him forever. He'd want you to love again."

Anna fought back tears. "But why does it have to be with someone who has no future here?"

Jessie smiled gently. "There's no stopping love."

Anna shook her head. "I have to think about Chloe now. She's so crazy about Noah already. She'll be crushed when he leaves." Anna drew in a breath and asked the question she dreaded. "Be honest with me. What are people saying about us?"

Jessie didn't answer right away, which meant her relationship with Noah was certainly fodder for community gossip. "You know how people talk. You shouldn't worry about what they say."

Anna lifted her chin. "I have to. Please tell me."

"Nothing that will surprise you. Everyone believes that he's an outsider who will never return to the community. He never joined the church, and he left the plain life behind. He chose another way."

Anna swallowed back her regret. "I know. Oh, Jessie, he's hurting so much, but I'm not sure why. I think it's because of my brother. You know how close Adam and Noah were. Losing his friend was hard for him."

Jessie nodded. "Maybe you're right. Perhaps Noah isn't the right one for you, but that doesn't mean there isn't someone out there. He might just be the tool Gött is using to open your heart to the possibility of loving again."

Anna tried not to show how impossible those words were to accept. Her heart belonged to Noah. There was no one else.

"Sir, can I have a word with you?" Noah was halfway back to the buggy where his Mamm, Anna, and Chloe waited for him when he realized one of the married men from church had followed him.

Noah turned back to the man. "Of course."

The young man appeared barely twenty. "My name is Samuel Yoder." He stuck out his hand, and Noah shook it.

"Nice to meet you, Samuel. What can I do for you?"

"I saw your flyer at the bulk food store. Are you still looking for help with the planting?"

Samuel's question surprised him. "Why, yes I am. Are you interested?"

He nodded eagerly. "Ja, I am. And so is my brother Michael. He wasn't able to be here today, but if you'd like, I could have him come by your place and talk with you."

"That would be nice. Where do you and your brother live?" Noah could see a young woman who was obviously pregnant waiting for Samuel in a modest buggy.

"My *Fraa* and I live with my Mamm and Daed outside of town. We are saving to buy our own place soon. Michael and I help my Daed with the farming."

Noah liked the young man right away. There was something about his honesty that struck a chord with him. "And is your brother married?"

"Nay, but he has plans to marry Faith Christner once the fall harvest is complete."

Noah smiled. "I see. Well, would it be possible for both you and your brother to stop by my farm tomorrow afternoon? You could take a look at the place, and we can come to an agreement."

Samuel beamed. "Ja, we can do that. I will see you tomorrow afternoon."

"Do you know where I live?"

The younger man nodded. "I do. We will be there tomorrow afternoon. Danki for the chance."

Once the young man had joined his wife, Noah strode toward his waiting family.

"What did Samuel need to speak with you about?" his Mamm asked.

Noah waited until he was in his seat before answering. "He and his brother spotted my flyer. He wants to come to work."

Mercy pressed her lips together. This wasn't her favorite subject. But he'd need help if they were going to get the fields planted in time.

"He's a good young man with a *Kind* on the way. He will make a good hand, and so will his brother, Michael." Noah finally realized why the young man seemed so familiar. He'd still been a child when Noah left Rexford.

"He and his brother are *gut* men," Mercy agreed reluctantly.

He patted his Mamm's hand. "I'm glad I have your approval."

As they headed toward the farm, something caught his attention in the distance.

Smoke.

"That's on our property." His Mamm had spotted the blaze as well.

Noah shook the reins hard, hurrying Esther along, his heart pounding crazily against his chest.

Nothing could have prepared him for the horrifying sight as they rounded the final bend. The barn was engulfed in flames.

He jumped from the buggy before it stopped and raced inside. Jenny, the family's other mare, was still in her stall.

"Noah!" Anna cried.

He barely registered the fear in her voice as he charged into the building. Already, the flames had destroyed a great deal of the barn. He pulled his shirt up over his nose and mouth and tried to gain his bearings as tears streamed down his face. The smoke was overpowering.

"Let me help you." He turned to see Anna standing in the doorway.

"Stay out. The fire is too dangerous. You have Chloe to think about. Go!"

He could only hope she'd listened as he pushed farther into the smoke. He spotted Jenny frantically pawing at her stall door. Noah rushed toward the horse, fighting his way past flames. A few minutes more and the barn would be nothing but embers.

He hurried to the stall and unlatched it. The mare reared on her hind legs, screaming.

"Easy, girl. Everything is going to be okay. Come with me." He held the mare's bridle and pulled her along behind him. In her terror, she fought him every step of the way.

Before they reached the safety of the outdoors, the wall next to the barn door collapsed, sending fire shooting all around. Jenny broke free and charged for the opening. Noah jumped out of the way before he was trampled.

He fell to the ground and the flames caught his coat. If he stayed here, he would die. He had to keep fighting. He struggled to his feet and stumbled outside.

The second he was free of the fire, he fell to his knees, coughing.

"Noah!" Anna ran to his side. She removed her cloak and started beating his clothes, which were on fire.

His arm was badly burned, the pain excruciating.

"You're hurt." Anna's face was grim.

"I'm okay," he tried to reassure her. His head reeled from what had happened. The blaze continued to burn behind him. "We need to keep the fire contained before the blaze takes out the house and everything else."

"I'll go call the fire department in Eureka," Anna told him.

"No, I need your help. We have to try to contain the fire. Mamm, take Chloe and go to the phone shanty. Call the fire department right away."

Mercy nodded and took up the reins, turning Esther around.

Noah rushed to the well and drew a bucket full of water. "We need more buckets."

"I'll get the ones from the house." Anna raced away while Noah carried the bucket of water to the fire and threw it on the flames, but it was a losing battle.

How would he and Anna save his home by themselves?

Then he spotted a line of buggies barreling toward the house. Just about everyone in the Rexford community had seen the fire and had come to help a neighbor in need.

It was the Amish way.

14

Anna grabbed three buckets from inside the house and rushed to the well. She saw the approaching buggies and choked back tears of gratitude.

Noah refilled his bucket and went to the fire once more.

While Anna filled the three buckets, the first buggy arrived. One of the deacons of the church, Caleb King, appeared at Anna's side. Soon ten men, including Mason Burkholder, who had helped Anna so many times since her husband's death, were lined up from the well to the blazing fire.

Samuel Yoder took one of the empty buckets from Anna's hands to fill. "We'll handle this, Anna," he said.

Anna stood back and watched as the men of the community worked in unison, one man handing the bucket to the next until it reached Noah, who threw the water on the blaze, and then the bucket was sent back while another one came forward. They repeated this process again and again until the Eureka Fire Department arrived.

Working alongside the Amish men, the fire department quickly had the blaze under control.

When there was nothing left but a smoldering mess, Noah surveyed the ruins. Not since he'd buried his brother had she seen him look so distraught.

The fire had seared through his coat sleeve. His arm was burned. She needed to get him help right away. "Noah, there is a medical person with the fire department. You need to have your arm examined."

He circled to face her, clearly exhausted and utterly forlorn. "How could this have happened?"

Anna would have given anything to be able to answer him. "I don't know, but we'll figure it out together. The barn can be replaced, and quickly if we hold a barn raising. Jenny is okay. We are all okay."

He gave a weak smile. "I know that's true, but it's hard to accept. So many bad things have happened to us without explanation."

Anna couldn't argue with that.

The fire chief came up to them. "I'm Phil Hendricks. The fire appears to be contained for now. Once the scene is safe, the fire marshal will come in and determine the cause of the fire. Until then, we'll have firefighters stationed here in case something reignites."

Noah shook the chief's hand. "I appreciate that."

The chief noticed Noah's injured arm and called over one of his men. "Williams here is a trained EMT. Let him have a look at that arm."

The EMT opened his medical bag and cut away Noah's coat and shirt. "You have a second-degree burn there." Once Williams had treated and bandaged the area, he said, "Keep that changed and the area clean. If infection sets in, you need to go to the emergency room right away. Do you know the signs?"

Noah nodded. He had to know basic first aid for his job.

The fireman moved away.

Anna studied Noah, frowning. He'd rushed into the burning barn without any concern for his own well-being, all to save a horse. If Jenny had perished, that would have been a tragedy, of course. But what if something had happened to Noah? The thought was almost more than she could bear.

Caleb came up to them, and Noah shook his hand. "Thank you for your help today. I can't imagine how bad things would have been without you."

"You are welcome. When you decide where you would like to build your new barn, we will come help you rebuild. Until then, the men of the community will come by and help with the cleanup."

She could see that Noah was humbled and moved by the offer. "Danki, that's very kind."

Caleb shook his head. "Mercy is part of our community, as are Anna and Chloe. It is our duty to look out for each other."

Caleb walked away, to be replaced by Samuel.

"I will come by tomorrow with my Bruder as we discussed. We can begin the plowing for you, and we would be happy to help with any cleanup."

Noah shook his head. "It's *gut* of you to offer, but some of my equipment was destroyed in the fire. I don't know if I have a job to offer you anymore."

"My Daed has equipment we can use. I'll bring the plows over along with a wagon to help with the cleanup."

"Danki, Samuel," Noah said quietly. He shook the young man's hand, and Samuel walked away.

"I'd almost forgotten what it means to be Amish," he said in a humbled tone.

Anna could see that it was difficult for him to speak. "That's why I love living here so much."

He nodded. "I can understand that. Would it be all right with you if Mamm stayed with you and Chloe for the time being?"

"Ja, of course." Something was worrying him, and fear swept through her. "What are you afraid of?" Seconds later, the truth dawned. "You think the fire was set deliberately. Oh Noah. Why? Why would someone do that?"

He shook his head. "Why would someone kill my brother and father? Why try to hurt you? They're all connected, Anna. I have to figure out why, and I have to do it quickly. The longer this person avoids justice, the more time they have to carry out more heinous acts."

She touched his arm. "We will get through this. You're not alone. You have the community, your family. Me."

He smiled down at her. "I can do anything as long as I have you by my side."

Joy soared in her heart, but she tried to muffle it. The future was still uncertain. That must be Noah's to decide.

Anna dropped her gaze. "I'm going to check on Mercy. Then we'll need to prepare some food for the workers. They must be exhausted."

"Anna, wait." He caught her hand when she tried to move away.

She would have given anything to know his thoughts.

"I...Danki," he murmured instead of what she desperately wanted him to say.

Disappointment made speaking difficult. She managed a smile, and he let her go. She made her way to the house, fighting back tears. Why did this have to be so hard? Why did loving Noah hurt so much?

Embers from the destroyed barn still glowed, keeping the darkness at bay. The sky was filled with millions of stars. If not for the suspicions gnawing at his insides, Noah would have been in awe of the beauty Gött had created. But he couldn't let go of the belief that the fire had deliberately been set. Another accident? No, he'd be a fool to believe the long string of misfortune that had bombarded his family could be anything but intentional now.

Two firefighters watched the remains of the fire. Noah brought out coffee to them. They'd begun to sift through the debris before dark.

So far, nothing suspicious jumped out, but there was no doubt in his mind that something would turn up to point to arson.

"Thanks for the coffee," one of the firefighters said.

"No problem. Do you need anything else?"

"No sir. This is much appreciated. Seeing how your community pulled together to fight the fire was inspiring. I wish more communities could be like that," the second firefighter told him.

Noah had to agree. He'd pushed aside the kindness, the forgiving way of the Amish people by leaving so long ago. Yet even when wronged, they still forgave. Which was why he struggled to understand how such a forgiving community could pass down such a harsh judgment as the shunning his brother had received. Was he missing something?

"Thanks," he said when he couldn't think of anything else to say. "If you need me, I'll be up at the house. Stop by anytime."

Noah headed back to his spot on the porch where he'd been trying to understand why someone would go to such great lengths—first to commit a murder, maybe two, and now arson? What were they after?

He didn't understand what was happening, but there was no doubt in his mind that it had something to do with the Miller property that his family had wanted to buy. And somehow or other, Edward Latham was involved.

Whoever was behind all this would keep coming after his family—of that he was certain. The only way to protect them was to find out what was going on.

Noah called Robert. He needed answers now. He had to find a way to put the pieces together to find the person who was trying to harm his family.

"Hey, Noah. I was just about to call you."

"What did you find out?"

"I did some more digging on Northern Montana Energy. Turns

out they have ties to some very bad people. The company is owned by a Martin Carlisle. He has a history of dirty deals and suspected violence, but no charges have ever stuck. He and his goons are bad news. They've been strong-arming people into selling their properties, and they're not above using criminal means."

In other words, the situation was far worse than Noah had feared.

"Have they been successful in finding oil, or is the company a front for something else?" Noah couldn't believe someone who had been guilty of such dirty business would choose to get into the oil business. Digging for crude wasn't always a home run.

"From all accounts, the company has struck gushers on several of the rigs they've erected. I don't know how familiar you are with the business, but it turns out Montana is in the middle of one of the biggest oil booms in modern history. Naturally, this bit of news would come to the attention of some shady characters looking to make an easy buck."

He'd had no idea his home state held such bounty. But then again, he hadn't really kept up with what was happening here. "So how does Edward Latham fit into all of this?"

Robert sighed. "I don't know yet. I still can't tie him to Northern, but the fact that their registered vehicle was at his house is concerning. I'm guessing he knows something."

"Keep checking for me, will you? This thing has become personal."

"What do you mean?"

"My family's involved." He slowly revealed the whole saga to his friend—everything about his past and what he suspected about both his brother's and father's deaths, the attack on Anna, and the barn fire.

"I had no idea. I'm sorry."

Words were hard to come by. "Thanks."

"Do you think we need to bring this to the sheriff's attention?" Robert asked.

"We need more to go on."

"I'll keep checking. I'm going to try and find out who Carlisle's man is in the area. There has to be someone. Carlisle doesn't like to get his hands dirty."

"Thanks, Robert. Find me something useful. Whatever reason Carlisle has for coming after my family, he appears to be stepping up the pace."

15

Anna was finishing up breakfast when she heard a car engine outside. She peeked out the window curtains. Edward was coming up the drive in his usual car rather than the SUV he'd driven on his last unannounced visit.

After everything that had happened recently and with Noah's assumptions, Anna didn't know what to do. Why was he here?

"Who is that?" Chloe asked when there was a knock at the door.

"My boss. Stay here with your Grossmammi. I'll go see what he needs." What other choice did she have?

Anna wrapped her cloak around her shoulders and went outside. Edward was pacing on her front porch. He appeared as if he'd aged ten years.

"Edward? What's wrong?"

"Oh, Anna, this is all my fault. All my fault." He sat in the swing, his hands covering each side of his head.

"What are you talking about? What's your fault?"

The troubled look in his eyes was frightening. "Anna—" He appeared to be about to say something more when he heard a buggy coming their way. *Noah.* Relief coursed through her. She didn't trust Edward any longer.

When Edward saw the buggy, he leaped to his feet and rushed to his car. Before Anna could stop him, he got in, backed out, and raced away. What had he been about to say to her? Would he confess his part in her family's troubles?

Noah ran up the steps to her side. "What did he want?"

"I'm not really sure." She told him what the man had said to her.

Noah paced the same path Latham had. "I don't like it. I thought it would be safe for you here, but now I believe you and Chloe should pack a bag. You and Mamm will come back to Mamm's house. The area is too isolated, and this is the second time that man has showed up unexpectedly. We should all be together."

Anna glanced back at the window where her daughter and Mercy watched them and lowered her voice. "Do you really think he's involved in what happened with the barn?"

He held her gaze. "I do."

She shuddered at those simple words. "I still can't believe he would do such a thing."

He took her hand. "Until we figure out what's going on here, I want you and Chloe close."

Anna understood the reason behind his concern. Something terrible was happening to their family. "What should I tell Chloe? She's going to wonder why we're coming to stay with you again."

His eyes scanned the yard. "We'll tell her that Mamm misses her home, but wants her family close after what happened with the barn. She loves her Grossmammi. She won't question it too much."

Anna nodded and went inside, followed by Noah.

As always, Chloe was happy to see her Onkel.

Noah crouched and gave her a bear hug. "How would you like for you and your Mamm to come stay with me and your Grossmammi at our house for a while?"

Chloe's eyes grew wide. "Can we, Mamm?" she pleaded.

Anna smiled. "Ja, we can. Your Grossmammi misses her home, so we're going to stay with her for a little while." Anna gave Mercy a meaningful look, and she nodded. She understood something was going on.

Chloe bounced in place, excited by the upcoming adventure.

"Let's go pack. We don't want to forget your doll, do we?" Anna asked.

Chloe shook her head.

Anna took Chloe's hand and headed toward her bedroom.

"How long can we stay there, Mamm?" Chloe asked.

Anna hoisted her suitcase down and placed it on the bed. "I'm not sure yet."

"Mamm, are you and Onkel Noah getting married?"

Shocked, Anna pivoted toward her daughter. "Why would you ask that?"

"I heard Grossmammi talking with her friend. She said she thought you might, and then Onkel Noah would stay here with us forever and ever. She said she could think of nothing that would make her happier."

Anna stopped what she was doing and sat on the bed near her daughter. "Chloe, your Onkel is a great man, but he has his own life outside of Rexford. He's happy to be here with us now and spend time with us, but someday he will have to leave again. He has a job waiting for him."

Tears welled in her daughter's eyes, spilling over and tearing at Anna's heart. "I don't want him to leave. I want him to stay with us."

Anna gathered her daughter close. *Me too, little one.* "I know this is hard to think about, but we wouldn't want him to stay when he has someplace else he's supposed to be, now would we? He keeps a lot of people safe, doing what he does."

Chloe didn't answer, tears streaming down her cheeks and sobbing as if her heart were breaking.

Anna held the girl until her tears subsided. Then she rose to her feet. "Now come on, dry those eyes. We have to finish packing. Onkel Noah is waiting. And I wouldn't want him to see that you've been crying. He would feel bad if he knew your tears were because he had to leave one day. We need to live for the moment, Chloe. Your Onkel is here with us now. Let's be happy with that."

As much as she wanted to believe what she said, she knew her heart would break like Chloe's when he was gone.

Anna stepped out on the front porch next to Noah and smiled. He smiled back and pretended that his breath was taken away by the line of buggies and wagons heading toward the house rather than her sparkling green eyes in the early morning light. Almost the entire community had come together to help Noah rebuild his family barn.

Anna and his mother had spent most of the previous day preparing food.

Several of the local men had come earlier in the week to lay the blocks and cement used in the foundation to allow time for it to dry and set.

Noah had been to enough barn raisings during his teenage years to know that the work would take a week or so to complete. But by the end of today, the wooden framework of the building would likely be completed.

Noah jumped off the porch to greet Caleb King, who had a wagon filled with building supplies.

"A beautiful day for a barn raising, don't you think?" Caleb asked.

"That it is," Noah agreed. If only he could shut out the troubles from his mind and enjoy the simple task of working with his hands.

"Let's get to work. If we want to have the frame in place, it will take every bit of daylight we can get."

Noah smiled and headed with Caleb toward the foundation.

"The men did a fine job of preparing the foundation," someone said.

Noah noticed furtive glances being thrown his way. He knew the community was buzzing with curiosity about him since his return. Several of the women were talking to Anna and looking meaningfully toward him. He couldn't imagine what their conversation would entail.

He spent the day working alongside Caleb, Mason, and Samuel, and he was proud of the work he did. He believed his father would have been as well.

The ladies had made a makeshift table of boards and sawhorses, which they covered with tablecloths, then copious amounts of food.

Exhausted in a good way, Noah caught Anna's eye and motioned her away from the crowd. They strolled to a quiet corner of the property. He wanted to tell her about what the fire chief had found.

"Is everything okay?" she asked when she glanced at his worried expression.

"I'm not sure. The fire chief called me this morning. He believes the fire was an accident. He said there was a lantern that was left burning in the barn close to Jenny's stall. She must have kicked it over."

Anna didn't break eye contact. "But you don't believe it."

He blew out a sigh. "No, I don't. I was the last person in the barn, and I'm positive I extinguished the lantern. I sure didn't leave a light anywhere near Jenny's stall."

"Another accident." She whispered his thoughts.

"Yes. They are mounting. Someone is trying to get to us. The only question is, why?"

It broke his heart to see the fear in her eyes. "What should we do?"

"Don't worry. I won't let anything happen to you or to Chloe."

She clasped his hand. "I know that, but if this keeps up, no one is safe. Not even the men working on the barn."

"You're right. Speaking of them, I'm so grateful for the way the community has welcomed me. It's more than I deserve."

She clearly didn't understand what he meant. "Why would you say that? Of course you deserve to be accepted. Rexford was once your home. It can be again if you choose."

He wished he could believe her.

Still, Gött must have led him back here for a purpose. Was it to make peace with the past once and for all? Was it time to face what had happened and accept the consequences, whatever they might be?

But what if he admitted the truth and lost Anna? She was such a warm, caring person, and he was falling in love with her. Maybe already had.

He roused himself. "This has been a long day, but we've made a lot of progress. The rest of the barn will go up easily enough, I think."

She smiled at him. "It will be a fine barn. Your Daed would be pleased with the work you've done."

He returned her smile. "I think he would too."

"Have you heard anything more from your friend?"

He shook his head. "Not recently, and I don't like the silence. Especially after Latham's visit. The man knows something." He thought back over everything Robert had told him. Suddenly, he remembered something. "Have you ever met the Lathams' son?"

Anna's eyes widened in surprise. "They have a son? They've never mentioned him before, and we've talked a lot."

"That's odd. He's lived here for what—seven years? You'd think his son would come to visit from time to time. Did the Lathams ever have visitors at the ranch while you were there?"

"I think he did."

Her answer was strange. "What do you mean, you think he did?"

"I caught a glimpse of someone once shortly before my accident.

Edward wasn't around when I arrived, only his wife. When I tried to clean the study, Edward met me at the door. There was another man in there seated with his back to me. I only saw him through the crack in the door. Edward told me he was in a meeting, and I could clean the room on my next visit. He didn't sound like himself. He was worried about something."

Her answer didn't sit well with him. "I wonder if that was the man who was at the Millers' old place. The one who drove the SUV. Have you ever heard Latham mention drilling for oil around here before?"

"No, never. Do you think what's happening has something to do with oil?"

He did, but he had no idea how. "There's no doubt Latham is connected to Northern Montana Energy somehow. I'm guessing the man who was visiting him was the same man who ran you off the road. Latham seems to have genuine affection for you, so I don't think he did it. I have to figure out how the two are connected before something else happens."

Anna gave him a brave smile. "You'll figure things out. I know you will."

Her confidence touched him. He peered into her eyes and wanted so much for her to be his. He moved close, only a whisper separating them. She didn't step away, didn't avert her gaze. The future was his to decide.

He stopped. She'd been hurt badly by Joseph's death. He couldn't hurt her again. If he stayed, the truth would inevitably come out about what he'd done. He wouldn't be able to hide anything from her. And then she would regret giving her heart to him. She'd hate him. How could he bear that?

He was afraid the past would stand between them forever. The decision he'd made that fateful day had destroyed more than Adam's life. It had left its mark on his, Joseph's, and Anna's.

He drew in a breath and stepped back. "We should probably get back to the others before more rumors are spread about us."

Color stained her cheeks and she quickly looked away from him. Did she think he didn't want to be tied to her? Nothing could have been further from the truth. He would have given anything to call her his own and love her for the rest of his life.

But she could never be his. The dark secret he harbored prevented anything of the sort.

16

As much as Chloe loved being with Noah and her Grossmammi, and as pleasant as it was for Anna too, Anna couldn't dispel the feeling that something bad was about to happen.

While Noah and the men of the community continued work on the barn, the Yoder brothers were busy planting the spring wheat crop.

Anna and Chloe spent their days helping Mercy plant her garden. Anna was grateful for the distraction of dirt and seeds. The activity helped to take her mind off the future.

After Edward's strange visit to her home, she was too afraid to go back to work for him. As much as she didn't want to believe he was capable of hurting the people she loved, she was sure he knew something about what happened and had tried to tell her. What would happen when she didn't show up at work? Would he come looking for her again, or would the man who'd run her off the road show up to finish the job?

While Anna hoed the row, Chloe dropped seeds in at regular intervals behind her. Her precision was quite good for a girl her age. They had been working for most of the morning.

"Let's take a break, you two," Mercy told them and wiped her forehead.

Anna straightened, her back aching from leaning over the hoe for hours on end. She scanned the ground they'd planted. They'd made a lot of progress.

"We're almost finished," she said in amazement.

Mercy nodded. "Let's go start lunch. We can finish up after the meal. Come, love." Mercy grasped Chloe's hand.

"I'm going to take the men some water," Anna said. "They have to be thirsty by now."

"That would be kind." Mercy smiled, and she and Chloe headed for the house.

Anna strolled to the well and drew a bucket of fresh water, then carried the bucket and the ladle toward the newly erected barn. She'd almost reached the men when, off in the distance, she spotted the same SUV that she now knew had been used to run her off the road.

She froze, and the bucket slipped from her hand. Noah must have heard the noise because he raced to her side. "Anna, what's wrong?"

She pointed to the vehicle.

"Go inside." He didn't wait for her answer. He strode toward the SUV.

"No! They could hurt you," she called after him, but he didn't stop. She watched in horror as the SUV thundered toward the man she loved.

At Noah's approach, the driver fired the engine, whipped the SUV around, and sped away.

Noah stopped and slowly headed back to where she stood.

"What do you think they want?" she asked, still shaking.

"I don't know." He peered into her eyes. "Anna, it's getting too dangerous around here. Whoever was in that vehicle is doing his best to intimidate us."

Anna didn't know what to say. "This is our home. We can't leave."

He appeared troubled. "We may not have a choice."

She bit her lip. "What do you want to do?"

He frowned, then seemed to come to a decision. "For now, you, Chloe, and Mamm need to stay out of sight as much as possible. No more gardening. And I will get in touch with my friend. We need help."

She glanced back at the house. "What do you want to tell your Mamm?"

Deep furrows lined his forehead. "I don't want to frighten her. For now, we should tell her that the man who ran you off the road is threatening you again. I don't want to bring what happened to Daed and Joseph into this yet."

She nodded. "All right. I'll go help Mercy with the meal preparation. If she asks me anything, I'll tell her to ask you."

"*Gut.* I'd better get back to work. We're almost done with the barn. The sooner we finish, the better. These men have been so kind and generous. I don't want to put them in the crosshairs of whoever is doing this to us. Once we're done, I'm going to call my friend again and see if he has any news for me."

She caught his hand. "Please be careful."

Noah's first instinct was to grab the cell phone and call Robert, but it would be disrespectful to do so in front of the Amish community who were helping him and his Mamm. He returned to the barn.

"Is there a problem, Noah?" Caleb called to him.

Keeping the truth from showing was hard. "No problem. I thought I recognized that vehicle. I was wrong."

"The driver appeared not to know you, I'd say." Caleb continued to pin him with those piercing eyes.

"I guess he didn't."

Caleb stepped away from the other two men, and Noah followed. He knew the man had much to say, but he wasn't so sure he wanted to hear.

"We are a peaceful community here at Rexford. We don't invite trouble. We know the type of danger you face in your English world."

Noah believed he knew what was coming next. "I know, Caleb. I'm not trying to bring trouble to the community. This is the last thing I want."

Caleb held up a hand. "Hear me out."

Noah held his tongue with difficulty. "Oke."

"While we are a peaceful group, we don't like when members of our community are threatened. We want to protect them as best we can."

Noah was shocked into silence. He couldn't think of a single thing to say.

"Lots of accidents seem to surround your family as of late. One has to think that perhaps not all of them have been accidents. While you may not be part of our community, your family is, and we wouldn't want anything to happen to them. If we can be of help, we are at your service."

Noah couldn't believe what he'd heard. Caleb's kindness was more than he deserved. "Danki, Caleb. I am honored by the offer."

Caleb held out his hand and Noah shook it. "You are welcome. We've finished the barn. Come see."

Noah noticed two men who had been working with them today putting away their tools. They'd completed the final touches while Noah and Caleb talked.

Noah followed Caleb to the barn. The craftsmanship that had gone into completing the building was remarkable. The Amish were known for their hard work and skill. Noah was proud to be a small part of the effort.

The barn that had burned was not nearly as large as the new one. There would be plenty of room for the horses and the buggy, as well as the crops gathered from this year's harvest.

"Danki," Noah told the men. "I couldn't have done this by myself. I owe you all so much. I don't know what to say to fully express my appreciation."

The men tipped their hats. "This is what our community does," one said simply. They headed for their wagons.

Caleb lingered.

Noah turned to him, sensing the elder had more to say.

"As I said, your family is important to our community. I know your brother endured a shunning that was a hardship for your family, but Joseph worked hard to restore the community's trust in him."

At the mention of his brother's shunning, Noah found keeping silent was impossible. "His punishment was more than he deserved."

Caleb smiled kindly. "Perhaps you don't know everything." He tipped his hat. "Good day to you, Noah. May Gött watch out for your family."

Noah watched Caleb climb into his wagon. As he watched the elder leave, his cell phone rang.

Only one person would be calling. "Robert. I was getting ready to call you."

"I'm on my way to your place as we speak. Is there someplace where we can meet? I'll be there in ten minutes."

"I'll meet you at the edge of town where the signs are. I can be there in ten."

"Good. Oh, and Noah, it's best if you don't tell anyone where you're going. This is big and best discussed in person. And you never know who might be listening."

Noah hated that he would have to leave without informing his family where he was going, but he could tell Robert had had a major breakthrough with the case. "I'll see you there."

Noah shoved the phone back into his pocket and went to where Jenny grazed. There wasn't time to harness the wagon. He hopped up on the mare's back, with a brief wish that he had time to saddle her, and nudged her toward the meet location, his thoughts churning with possibilities. It was only after he was halfway to town that he realized he'd taken the horse automatically, hadn't even thought about his car. But there was no time to think about what that meant now.

As he rushed toward town, his fear for his family's safety escalated. He hated leaving them alone. But Anna was smart. She'd do what she had to do to protect Mamm and Chloe. And he didn't intend to be gone long.

Once he reached the place where the signs indicated the location of the businesses, Noah tied Jenny to the signpost. A dark sedan was parked close by. He headed that way, and the driver's door opened.

Robert climbed out of the driver's seat, followed by Noah's commander, Eric Stephens. The fact that his boss was here proved the seriousness of the situation.

"I take it you've discovered something?" Noah asked.

"We have, and the situation is far more serious than we thought," his commander said. He held open the back passenger door. "Let's talk inside."

The severity of the situation was frightening. Noah climbed inside, the commander next to him.

Robert got behind the wheel, and the commander handed Noah a file.

"What's this?" Noah asked.

"This is what we've found out about the man you had us check on. Carlisle's company has been secretly buying up Amish farmland around the area. They've discovered oil on the Miller place. A lot of it, in fact, as well as on the surrounding farms. Carlisle has Latham's son doing his dirty work. He's been threatening the Amish people, trying to strong-arm them into selling."

Noah couldn't believe what he was hearing. "Did they force Mrs. Miller to sell out?"

"They did. But whether or not they used deadly force is uncertain. She died shortly after signing the contract, supposedly from a heart attack, but in light of everything else, I'm planning to investigate further."

Had Mrs. Miller been killed like his Daed and brother?

"We believe that the largest amount of the oil deposit may be located under your family's farm," Robert told him. "They probably believe that too. They can't legally pump the oil without your consent, and they don't want to risk you giving that consent on condition that you get some of the profits from the oil. We believe they've been trying to force your family to sell for a while. When your family refused, the company resorted to deadly force, hoping that the next member of your family would be more reasonable. I'm guessing that's what happened with your dad and brother. I imagine they will approach either your mother or your sister-in-law next. I believe the staged accidents and acts of vandalism piling up are also a way to make your family not want to live on the farm anymore anyway. If they believed too much had gone wrong, they might even be eager to sell."

Noah couldn't believe the depths to which Carlisle and his team were willing to stoop. "And you believe that Eddie Latham was the one responsible?" Noah's hands tightened into fists as he fought back rage. "Where's Carlisle in all of this? Where's he hiding out?"

"Carlisle is hiding across the border in Canada where he has a home, although he has been spotted in the area from time to time. We have him under surveillance. His base of operations is located on the Latham ranch. Eddie is there. We're raiding the Miller place tonight at the same time we go after the Latham ranch. We need you back on this one, Noah," Eric said quietly. "You know the community and the layout of the land. We need your help."

"Anything to keep my family safe." *Anything to keep Anna safe.*

17

"Anna, why don't you go tell Noah it's time to eat?" Mercy said once they had finished putting the food on the table.

Anna stepped outside. She'd seen Noah and Caleb talking earlier before Noah received a call. Now, he was nowhere in sight. He must be in the new barn. She headed that way and realized that Jenny wasn't in the field where she'd seen her earlier. The barn was empty. Where was Noah?

She left the barn, her eyes surveying the area. In the distance, a horse and rider headed her way. As he drew closer, she saw it was Noah. Where had he been?

As he neared, the expression on his face sent a shiver down her spine. She fought to keep her emotions in check as Noah dismounted.

"You're leaving." She forced the words out.

His expression was raw and haggard. "I'm sorry, but I've been called back on a mission. I have to do this, Anna. For you and Chloe and Mamm."

"What are you talking about?"

"I can't go into the details, but it has to do with what happened to my Daed and Joseph. Please try to understand. I have to do this."

"Why you? Why can't someone else handle it this one time?"

"This is personal."

Anna slowly nodded. There would be no changing his mind. "When do you leave?"

A dark sedan pulled into the drive, and Noah glanced behind him at it. "Now. But I'll be back. I promise I will and when I am, we have a lot to talk about." His expression begged her to understand. "Anna, I . . . I care about you."

She stepped back. There were so many things to say, but the words wouldn't come. She was already trying to distance herself from what was happening. "You must do what you have to do. Goodbye, Noah." She spun and strode to the house, ignoring his calls to her. She wouldn't look back. He didn't deserve to see her heart breaking.

Noah waited until the sedan came to a stop, then climbed inside. He hated that he had to leave Anna without telling her why, but he was sworn to secrecy.

"We have Eddie Latham in custody, and he's talking," Eric told him as he drove. "My men spotted him at the Miller place and took him in. He was trying to destroy evidence. I need you in on the interview, Noah. I want to nail Carlisle for his part in this."

Noah's thoughts spun. Things were happening so quickly. "What has Latham told you so far?"

"That he's in debt to Carlisle. That's how he became involved with the man in the first place. Carlisle demanded he pay back the money he owed. He couldn't, so he had to try to find another way. A survey was done on his parents' property that proved there were oil-rich pools under the property, but the biggest reservoir was located under the Amish community. Carlisle had no problem destroying the community to get what he wanted."

"Unbelievable," Noah said. "Did he say anything about my family yet?"

Eric eyed him. "Not yet. I need you focused, Petersheim."

He steeled himself. His family was depending on him. "I'll be fine."

They arrived at the ranch and drove around to the back. "Eddie's called Carlisle and asked him to meet him here. He told him there was a problem. Once he arrives, we have him. And from all the information in the files, he's going away for a very long time."

They got out of the car and entered one of the buildings behind the house.

In the middle of the room, Eddie Latham stood surrounded by agents. When Noah approached, Eddie took a step backward.

When he saw the man who had murdered his Daed and Joseph, something snapped inside Noah. He wanted nothing more than to scream at the man and terrify him into spilling his secrets, just as he had terrified Noah's people into giving up their homes.

But he must remain calm. He couldn't do anything to jeopardize the court case. The last thing his family needed was for the defense lawyer to be able to argue that the confession had been coerced and was therefore inadmissible. "Did you kill my brother and my father?" he asked, in as cool a voice as he could muster.

"I had no choice," Latham whined. "It was them or me. Carlisle told me he would kill me if I didn't get your property. I believed him. He's a bad man."

"Tell me what happened."

Latham explained how he went to Joseph with the idea to buy the property for more than its value, but Joseph refused. Carlisle came up with the idea to kill him and Henry. He hadn't expected or known about Noah. Carlisle believed once Henry and Joseph were out of the picture, then he could convince the women to sell.

"Why would Carlisle think my mother and Anna would sell our home? We've owned the property for years."

Latham appeared uncomfortable. "He had someone on the inside, someone from the community watching Anna. He was supposed to be hinting that she should sell."

Someone from the community watching Anna.

Then it clicked. Mason Burkholder. Anna had said how helpful he'd been before Noah arrived. That would be the perfect cover for keeping an eye on her. Noah's thoughts went back to the footprints he'd seen around the barn the night he'd arrived and the broken window at Anna's home. His gut told him that had been Mason. But where was the man now?

Noah faced Eric, fear in the pit of his stomach. "I need to get out of here. My family's in danger."

Eric nodded to Robert, who tossed the sedan's keys to Noah. "We'll be right behind you."

Noah raced out of the building and climbed into the car. He put the vehicle in drive and floored the gas pedal.

18

Anna had almost finished hanging out the laundry when someone stepped up behind her.

"I'm just finishing up, Mercy." She whirled and gasped.

It wasn't Mercy. It was Mason Burkholder.

Her heart pounded in her chest. "Mason, what are you doing here?"

He stepped closer. "You should have listened to me. If you'd agreed to let me sell the place, nothing would have happened to you. I have to do this, Anna. I owe him, and he always gets what he wants."

She glanced down to catch her breath and saw something reflecting the sunlight in his hand.

A knife.

Somehow her voice was calm and low. "Who wants you to do this? Mason, did you hurt Joseph?" Her heart clenched at the betrayal.

Mason pointed to the house. "Get inside. I have to make it look like an accident."

"Please, you don't have to do this. I know someone who can help you." Why had Noah had to go on that mission now?

He gave her a shove toward the house. "No one can help me. He has my family. He's going to kill them if I don't do this today."

The fear in his eyes sent her heart racing. "Oke, I'm going."

He stared around nervously. "Hurry up. I don't have long. He has to meet with Latham soon."

Anna's thoughts scattered. *Latham.* Was Edward involved after all?

She stepped up on the porch and hurried inside. She couldn't let anything happen to Chloe or Mercy, but what was she going to do?

"Anna, did I hear you talking to someone?" Mercy stopped when she spotted the knife in Mason's hand. "What's going on here?"

"Just do as he says, Mercy," Anna said.

Mercy gathered Chloe close. The fear in her daughter's eyes was more than Anna could bear. She'd die before she'd let her child be harmed.

Mason pointed the knife at the great room. "Get over there." They hurried into the great room, where he tossed some rope to Anna. "Tie them up."

With fear coursing through her body, she tied Mercy and Chloe together.

"Mamm, I'm scared," Chloe whimpered.

"Everything is going to be okay. I'm not going to let anything happen to you," Anna said, praying it wasn't a lie.

Mason had some paper in his hand. He stuck it into the woodstove, then carried the flaming paper to the curtains and torched them.

Chloe screamed.

"No one's going to believe this was an accident, Mason," Anna said quickly, trying to get him to see reason. "Not after the fire in the barn. Did you set that as well?"

She could see the truth in his eyes.

"I didn't have a choice. I owe him money. I promised I'd get your farm for him. I tried to do it without hurting you, but now he's going to hurt my family if I don't take care of you." He snatched one of the lanterns and threw it on the blazing curtains, where it exploded and the fire roared up.

Anna couldn't let him tie her up. She waited until he was distracted by the fire. Then she snatched the fireplace poker, prayed for forgiveness, and whacked Mason over the head with the poker. He dropped to the ground, unconscious.

She raced to untie Mercy and Chloe, who were coughing. "Get outside," she wheezed. "Mercy, get some water to put out the fire. I'm going to try and drag Mason out of here."

"He's too heavy for you alone. Let me help."

Anna knew that by helping her, Mercy's home stood the chance of being destroyed for good. But she couldn't let the man die. It wasn't their way.

"Go outside now, Chloe. We'll be right behind you."

With another fearful look at the fire, Chloe rushed out the door.

"Take one of his legs," Anna told Mercy. Together they grabbed the unconscious man's legs and struggled every step of the way until they got him out of the house.

Anna snatched the rope he'd intended to use on her and tied his hands and legs. Then she ran to the well and drew a bucket of water. Working with Mercy, they each took turns drawing water to toss on the fire, but it was useless. The blaze was out of control. Soon the entire house was engulfed.

Mercy's eyes brimmed with tears. Anna couldn't imagine how hard it must be for her to lose her family home. Her life with Henry had been here. She'd watched her children grow up here. Everything she owned and knew was here.

Anna hugged her close. "I'm so sorry."

Mercy brushed her eyes and drew Chloe close. "It will be all right. The house can be replaced. We're safe. That's all that matters."

Behind them, they heard the sound of a vehicle approaching. Anna spotted the same sedan that had raced away with Noah.

The vehicle screeched to a stop and Noah jumped out and ran toward them. "Anna, are you all right? What happened?"

"We're all okay," Anna reassured him. "Mason said someone wanted him to. He said they have his family."

Noah stared at the house, and Anna imagined that he felt much the same way Mercy did.

"Soh, it's no use. There's no saving the house," Mercy told him quietly.

Mason groaned as he regained consciousness.

Noah hauled the other man to his feet. "Did Carlisle tell you to do this?"

Mason nodded, tears streaming down his face. "They have my family. They'll kill them."

"Where?" Noah asked.

"At my house. They warned me if I don't get the job done in an hour, they'll kill them. That time is almost up."

Noah whipped out his phone and called in the fire to 911. Then he dialed Robert. "Mason Burkholder's family is being held hostage at the Burkholders' home. Get there quickly." Mason told him the address, and Noah relayed the information to Robert. "I have Burkholder here. He set the fire, but thank God my family is safe."

Anna came to stand beside Noah, who still kept a watchful eye on Mason. She took his hand and he turned to her. "I was so afraid I would lose my family. I couldn't bear the thought."

She gave him a weak smile. "We're okay. But your house. I'm so sorry."

He stared at the blazing fire and then back at her. "It's a house. As long as you are all safe, we can rebuild."

Eric and Robert arrived shortly after the fire department had put out the blaze, having taken Edward Latham's car with his permission.

"Mason's family is safe, and Carlisle is in custody," Eric told Noah.

He'd sent his Mamm with Chloe and Anna to Anna's house to stay for a while. There was nothing they could do now.

"The sheriff has taken Mason into custody," he told his commander.

Eric nodded. "As far as we can tell, his crimes are arson and attempted murder. The DA may cut him a deal if he testifies against Carlisle and Latham."

Noah couldn't imagine what the man had gone through, knowing his family's lives depended on him harming someone else. Even with all Noah's skills and training, he knew anyone who threatened his family would put him much in the same helpless position. "He was only trying to protect his family. I don't see my family pressing charges outside of whatever the prosecutor brings. Forgiveness is the Amish way."

He knew Anna had already forgiven Edward Latham Senior, who had known what his son had planned the night she was run off the road and had tried to warn her. He hadn't succeeded, but he hadn't been able to bring himself to out his son. Noah didn't agree with his choice, but he understood it.

And now the men responsible for all the trouble his family had gone through were in custody and would face justice. He breathed deeply, feeling lighter than he had in as long as he could remember.

"I'm sorry about your family. I know words won't bring him back, but your dad would be proud to know you helped bring his killer to justice."

"Thanks," he murmured. And in a flash, he knew what else would please his Daed and set his own heart at ease. It was time to face up to his past. He would bear the consequences, whatever they were. "Eric, this is it for me. I've struggled with the decision for a long time, but I want to return to my Amish roots. I'm done with the spy game."

Eric didn't appear the least surprised. "I can't talk you out of it?"

"I'm afraid not. I belong here."

Eric gave him a small smile and shook his hand. "I'm sad to see you go, but I get it. If this doesn't work out for you, you'll always have a job with me."

"Thanks." He said goodbye to Eric and Robert and watched them leave. They passed a buggy heading his way.

Anna.

She stopped the buggy next to him, and their eyes met.

He reached up and put his hands around her waist, then lifted her to the ground.

"I'm glad you came," he said honestly. She was so beautiful. And alive.

"Who was that?" she asked as the vehicle left.

"My commander." Noah drew in a breath and laid his heart bare. "I told him I'm done with the English life. I don't want to be a spy any longer."

She hesitated, as if preparing herself. "What *do* you want?"

"You. I know it's only been a year since Joseph's death, and you may need more time, but I love you, Anna, and I want to marry you. I'll wait as long as you need. I want to spend the rest of my life with you, right here where I belong, in Rexford." He stopped for a breath. "But you have to know something first."

He let her go and put distance between them, praying she wouldn't hate him.

"Joseph lied when he said Adam was at fault when Adam fell through the ice that day. I started some stupid argument with him, and he pushed me. I fell on the ice, and it cracked. He shoved me out of the way, only to fall through the ice himself, and I couldn't reach him to pull him back out. He died saving my life. I am responsible for your brother's death, not Joseph, and I need your forgiveness. I want to join the church and become a member of the community, but first I have to set this right and clear Joseph's name, even if it means I will be shunned. I'll do everything in my power to make that right as well," he finished in a rush of words, his fear of what she'd say taking his breath away.

For the first time ever, he couldn't read her expression. What was she thinking?

After a horrible silence, she asked quietly, "Is that why you left?"

"Yes. I couldn't face it. I had ruined so many lives. I thought I should leave before I ruined any others. I chose to work as a spy because I felt that they were protecting people, and I owed that to Adam's memory."

She didn't speak again for a long time, during which Noah watched her with his heart in her hands. What if he had lost her? He deserved it after causing her brother's death, but he didn't know if he could bear it.

Finally, she looked up at him, and the peace in her eyes told him he had made the right decision. "It wasn't your fault, Noah. You shouldn't have argued with him, but I am proud to know my brother gave his life for his friend. He truly loved you. But if you think you need my forgiveness, you have it. And there's something you should know." She touched his cheek gently. "Joseph's shunning didn't have anything to do with Adam's death. The bishop and elders understood that was an accident. Joseph stole money from Adam."

Nothing could have prepared Noah for that. "What are you talking about? What money?"

Anna sighed deeply. "Adam was supposed to buy seed wheat for our family later that day, and he had the money to pay for the wheat in his bag. Joseph innocently took the bag home with him after the accident. The day was crazy, and he wanted something to remember Adam by. Later, he found the money and kept it, but returned the bag. But a few days later he realized it was wrong, and he brought it back to my parents' house and left it there when we weren't home. But what he'd done bothered him, and he finally confessed to the elders. That's why he was shunned, and why it was for a brief time. What he did was wrong, though he had only been thinking of your family. The decision had nothing to do with Adam's death."

"Why didn't my parents tell me this before?" He didn't understand.

"They didn't want you to think badly of Joseph. They felt he had been punished enough."

Noah shook his head. "I wish I had known. I wouldn't have thought badly of Joseph. I loved him."

"He knew you loved him." She smiled up at him with tears glistening in her eyes. "Believe me, he knew. You have always had so much love to give. It's one of the reasons I've fallen in love with you."

And with those words, he was finally free.

"I love you, Anna." He leaned down and kissed her. Her lips were everything that he'd dreamed of, and he couldn't wait for their life together to begin, and for the past and all its troubles to fade away to where it belonged at last—in the past.

19

"Welcome home, Fraa."

A year later, Noah opened the door to the home he had built for her, and Anna gasped with delight. She'd married the man she loved with all her heart, and they were moving into a new home to start their life together.

Today was the first time she'd seen the place. Noah had been working hard for months to get it ready, and he had refused to let her see it until he'd finished the place.

The prospect of building a new home on the same spot where'd she lost so much had been too hard for Mercy, at least for now. They had turned Anna's old home into her *Grossdawdy Haus*, and Anna and Chloe had lived with her until Noah finished their new house on the spot where so many memories were buried. "It's right that you should have the main house anyway, for your family," Mercy had told them.

Anna stepped inside, her eyes darting from the great room to the kitchen. Fine woodwork gleamed back at her everywhere she looked. A perfect new home in which to create their own memories. "It's beautiful, Noah," she whispered.

"I'm glad you like it. I've made plenty of room in case our family grows. I think Chloe dislikes being an only child."

Her heart swelled at how he always thought of others first. Aloud, she said, "Chloe would love to have a baby Bruder or *Schweschder*. She's so jealous of all of Jessie's children."

Noah chuckled and kissed her once more. At times, it was hard to believe that a year had passed since that terrible day when the truth had become clear. She still couldn't understand the depth of ugliness people would go to for greed. But she'd forgiven and made her peace. She even continued cleaning the Lathams' ranch. Edward was distraught by what his son had done, and he and his wife had done everything they could to make it up to Anna, though she had forgiven them readily. After all, this was the Amish way.

When the deadly activities that Northern Montana Energy Company had been involved in had come to light, the business lost most of its investors and was facing bankruptcy. She'd heard that some of the Amish families who had sold their properties were working with English lawyers to try to buy their land back. Some had just moved on.

And the oil? Anna and Noah had decided that it could stay right where it was. They had no need for the wealth that drilling on their property might bring.

Although they had lost people dear to them and been through so much, Gött had been there with them and had blessed them. They had each other, their health, their family, and their faith. That was more than enough for anyone.